Have You Seen This Girl?

Flocksdale Files, Book One

By Carissa Ann Lynch

Have You Seen This Girl?

Limitless Publishing, LLC
Kailua, HI 96734
www.limitlesspublishing.com

Formatting: Limitless Publishing

ISBN-13: 978-1-68058-275-8
ISBN-10: 1-68058-275-5

Dedicated To:

The missing. The lost. The forgotten. The addicted. The abused. The outcasts. And to the song lyrics that inspired Wendi's story –"The End" *by The Doors.*

Prologue

Present Day

I lost my straw three hours ago, which sucks because it was my favorite one. Getting up to look for it seems like a painstaking, insurmountable task right now, but I pull myself up to a sitting position and swing my legs over the side of the bed. The "bed" is nothing more than a dingy, rust-colored mattress that lies on the floor of a two-room basement apartment in Albuquerque, New Mexico.

The threadbare carpet that covers the floor provides no support for my feet, and frankly, it stinks. I get down on my knees and lay my face flat against the carpet, holding my breath and peering under an ancient, stained armchair and the dresser that stands beside it. Now, where the fuck is that straw?

All I can see are dust bunnies, mouse droppings, and the carcass of a cockroach. No straw. I let out a frustrated groan. I give up searching, stand back up, and pad across the hall to the tiny bathroom I share with my current boyfriend, Michael, or "Mick" when he thinks he's cool. I plop down on the toilet, running my hands through my tangled mop of greasy black hair.

I wait for the pee to come. Then wait some more. I can remember one of my old AA mentors, telling me once why opiates interfere with bodily functions like peeing, for instance. It was something about wires in the brain getting crossed...I wish I had a stopwatch to time this affair, but then it finally comes and I let out a sigh of relief.

Mick's clothes from the night before are strewn across the bathroom floor at my feet. Suddenly I have a thought, and begin rummaging through the pockets of a brown pair of khaki shorts that I remember him wearing last night. I find what I'm looking for: a tattered black wallet, worn out from age and being sat on all day long. I open it up and peer inside. It only contains two dollars, but that's fine by me—all I need is one.

Pulling out the faded, crumpled bill, I smooth it flat against the round edges of the wash basin. Once flattened, I begin slowly rolling it into a perfectly cylindrical mini-version of my straw. It's basically perfect.

The dope is in my bedroom drawer, along with my razor. Using the tiny blade, I lovingly chop the heroin until it is fine and powdery, and then use the rolled up dollar bill to suck it straight up my nose. Its taste hits the back of my throat instantly and drains down through my sinuses, a sensation I used to loathe but have grown to love.

Wiping the residue from my nose noisily with the back of my hand, I glance at Mick, who is still passed out on the bed. Getting high makes him sleepy, but it fills me with an insatiable need to do something productive.

Our bedroom is dotted with tiny land mines of crumpled t-shirts, inside-out jeans, and day-old panties. I make my way around the room, picking them up and tossing them all into a wicker laundry basket in the corner.

Besides the bedroom and bathroom, we have a small, windowless sitting area, a narrow galley kitchen, and a small extra bedroom that we use for trash and other random items. I move my cleaning to the living room, gathering up snack wrappers and empty Solo cups, and then carry them into the small silver garbage can under the kitchen sink. The sink is filled to the brim with two-day-old dishes, so I start filling the sink with water and shampoo.

I've been out of dish soap for weeks now, but the hair care product seems to get the job done so I don't complain. The water from the faucet never gets hot because our gas got shut off months ago. If I want hot water, I have to boil it. This all sounds ridiculous, I know. This is the twenty-first century, but my addiction has me back in the Stone Age, because when you're an addict, you don't spend money on things like food, water, clothes, electricity…you spend it on drugs. At least the truly hardcore addicts like me do.

Crusty teacups, sauce-covered plates, and sour-smelling utensils permeate the water, rising steadily to the brim. I plunge my hands into the frigid, cloudy water and begin mindlessly washing.

For the past six months, our daily life can be divided into three segments: looking for money to buy heroin, finding the drug, and then getting high. Oh, I almost forgot about the fourth segment: coming down from the drug—my least favorite time of day. Our entire life revolves around heroin and our bodies rely on it to function. It's not about getting "high" anymore because I never feel lifted or high-spirited, or overly *anything* these days. We wake up feeling low and we need it to feel normal. Maybe they should change the expression to "getting normal" or "avoiding feeling like shit," instead of "getting high."

Today will be different though. Today I have a date with my good friend rehab, and six hours from now, my daily routine should change dramatically. Mick isn't going, but I'm fine with that. He'll do his own thing when he's ready. I've been planning this for a month now, and finally the phone call came: a bed opened up at the local in-patient clinic and today is the day to report.

I've been to rehab before, and will mostly likely go again after this stint, but everything is about to change. This time around, major plans have been made for when I get out of rehab.

Those plans involve me and a sharp set of butcher knives, but I'll explain that later.

Perhaps you're wondering how I got this way. Or perhaps you don't give a damn. Either way, this is my story. It's not a story about addiction. This is a story about murder.

PART ONE

Chapter One

The Beginning

Eight Years Ago...

I was three minutes shy of turning thirteen. At the time, my name was Wendi Wise—my real name, by the way.

Every year my parents threw me a party. Not just any old party, either. They invited family and friends, my mom ordered a cake, and I got tons of presents. There were usually balloons, party favors, and dancing...

This year was different though. I'd insisted on not having a party this year. I was too mature for that childish nonsense. I was, after all, a teenager. Well, almost a teenager. My only request for my birthday this year was to go to the movies with my

5

best friend, Claire, and Claire's older sister, Samantha. I didn't actually want Samantha to go, but my mom insisted because she still thought Claire and I were too young to go anywhere by ourselves. Samantha wasn't that much older than us, only seventeen. She certainly didn't act older than us.

But it didn't matter anyway because our real plan was not to attend the theater, but to meet up with Joey and Zeke at the mall the theater was connected to. Like us, Samantha was also planning to skip the movie for a hook up with a boy, but she would be going off on her own to do it, which was fine by me and Claire. Our plan was to go our separate ways as soon as Claire and Samantha's mom dropped us off in front of the plaza. The three of us planned to meet back up at 10:30 p.m., which was thirty minutes before their mother planned on picking us up. The plan should go off without a hitch as long as we all paid attention to our watches and met back up as planned.

Claire's mom screeched to a halt in front of the Riverside Plaza. She gave us her whole drawn-out spiel about not talking to strangers, walking straight to the theater, and sticking together. As soon as we walked through those double glass doors, we defied every single one of her suggestions.

"See you dweebs back here at 10:30 sharp," Samantha commanded, giving us both a warning glance. Samantha was curvy and boisterous, with a perfect set of breasts and legs that went on for days. She had a way of commanding attention when she entered a room, but despite her lovely looks, she didn't have the personality to match. She was known for giving girls at school a good thumping whenever they questioned her authority.

There was no doubt that if we got her in trouble she would thump both of our asses too, no questions asked. She took off for the escalators to meet her beau, shaking her rump audaciously.

Claire and I looked at each other anxiously. "Ready?" she asked, trying her best to sound casual. I nodded excitedly. Joey and Zeke were two slightly older boys we met this past year. My father would describe them as misfits. They came from broken homes, dressed like thugs, and probably got suspended from school. That is, when they went to school.

Our parents would totally freak if they knew we were meeting up with them tonight. Joey and Zeke's reputations should have made them undesirable candidates when it came to choosing our boyfriends. But it was their rebellious nature itself that lured us there, and resulted in lying to our parents. I didn't want to tell Claire my true fears, which were that I half expected them to stand us up tonight.

We met Joey and Zeke nearly six months ago, on a previous visit to the plaza…That day, Claire and I had accompanied my mom on a shopping trip.

While my mom scoped out the entire Lane Bryant store, she gave us some money to use in the food court.

"Wanna get high?" asked a tall, lanky boy with white-blond hair from behind us. I wasn't even sure

if I knew what he meant, but he was older and handsome, with a contagious, joker-like smile. He told us his name was Joey and we followed him to the other side of the food court, where we met his quieter, but equally cute friend Zeke. Zeke was his polar opposite, with coal black scraggly hair, and a shorter, but brawnier, frame.

"We have to get back to meet her mom," Claire warned, biting at her fingernails nervously. "We'll have you back in less than five minutes. If she comes looking for you, just say that you had to use the shitter or something," Joey said, waving us away from the food court. We followed them, unsure of what we were getting ourselves into, but excited nevertheless.

Up until recently, Claire and I had always considered ourselves "good girls." There were girls in our classes at school who were known to be wild sexually, and they got into trouble with older boys. We always claimed to dislike those types of girls, but maybe, deep down, we secretly yearned to be reckless and carefree too.

So, we followed the boys. Perhaps that was our first major mistake.

The boys walked at a rapid pace, and my short, chubby legs struggled to keep up with them. It didn't take long for me to realize where we were headed. They were taking us outside of the mall.

"Wait. We can't leave with you guys. We're not even supposed to be out of the food court!" I protested, suddenly feeling uncomfortable and mildly afraid.

"We're not leaving the plaza. We're just going

to the side of the building to get high behind the bushes. We better hurry if we want to get back in time," Joey warned, taking my hand and pulling me along.

Claire had a panicked look on her face, but she trailed along behind us. Joey didn't let go of my hand. He gripped it tightly in his as we walked through the exit doors and slid behind the bushes at the side of the building. It was the first time I'd ever held hands with a boy.

It wasn't what I expected; my hands were cold and clammy, and his palms were rough with calluses. But there was something about pressing my hand into his that filled me with exhilaration. A rhythmic buzz pulsated throughout my entire body.

The four of us were strangers, but we huddled together closely, hidden by the thick shrubbery that surrounded us, creating our own little cave. Joey released my hand and fished out a pack of Marlboros from a side pocket on his loose fitting Tommy Hilfiger jeans. I wondered how a boy like him could afford such an expensive pair of jeans.

He pulled out a loosely rolled cigarette, but that wasn't what it was at all. He lit the end of it, and my nostrils were instantly filled with a powerfully noxious, skunk-like aroma. He was smoking marijuana!

He took several small puffs and passed the joint to me first. I wanted to look cool, so I put my lips on the tip of it and sucked deeply. A burning sensation hit the back of my throat, and I coughed uncontrollably over and over again. I expected Joey to laugh but he just smiled at me sweetly and patted me on the back. *"Next time, try taking small puffs,"* he coaxed sweetly. *I nodded, still struggling to catch my breath.*

Claire took a hit next, and then Zeke gave her something called a "shotgun," which was just him blowing smoke into her mouth. The way Claire stared into his eyes yearningly I knew they were hitting it off, just like me and Joey.

"We need to get back now," I said, suddenly hit with a spacey, slightly disoriented feeling. The fear and excitement I'd felt earlier was replaced with a new sensation: a mixture of adrenaline and headiness. "We have to go too. Can you guys walk yourselves back to the food court?" Joey asked, searching my eyes with a look of concern. I nodded, grinning giddily.

"Do you guys want our cell phone numbers?" Zeke asked, looking right at Claire. We both replied "Yes" in unison. Joey pulled a black Sharpie pen out of his pocket, scrawled his number on my left palm, then handed the pen to Zeke so he could do the same for Claire. Joey never took his eyes off mine. I stared back at him intently.

There were boys at school I was attracted to, but I'd never felt anything like this. I was afraid of his edginess, but enthralled by it too. We said our goodbyes, and then Claire and I took off, running through the mall frantically to get back to the food court. We should have been panicked, but we were flying high, laughing excitedly as we ran.

Lucky for us, my mom wasn't there, but it was less than a few minutes later that she showed up, towing an armful of Lane Bryant bags with her, clueless about our recent escapade. We rode home in silence, Claire and I smiling back and forth at each other nervously. I kept my hand at my side and my palm exposed, careful not to smear the number written across it.

That was six months ago. Our communications with Zeke and Joey since then had been via talking and texts over the phone. I'd begged my mom repeatedly to take me to the plaza again, but she had insisted I couldn't go alone until my thirteenth birthday. Claire's mom insisted on the same thing. I often thought our mothers were conspiring together.

So, here we were…back at the place where it all started, getting ready to see the boys again. My conversations with Joey had been short and aloof. He seemed different over the phone than in person, less friendly.

I simply couldn't contain my excitement as I followed Claire to the food court. I was nervous about seeing them again, but my heart was racing with excitement too. That's when I spotted him, standing in front of a small Arby's kiosk. My belly instantly filled with a fluttering sensation.

The boys seemed happy to see us again. Not only was Joey as amiable as the first time we'd met, he was even friendlier. The four of us ate roast beef sandwiches and played on the scooters in Toys R Us until one of the managers asked us to leave. We ran out of the store, chuckling amongst ourselves and nodding at each other goofily.

After that, Joey and Zeke offered us more pot, and we obliged, returning to our secret hiding spot.

I took more puffs this time around, and my head felt confused and my belly woozy. Last time, I'd felt giddy when I smoked it. But this time it was too much. I instantly didn't want to be high anymore.

But then Joey did something that eased all of my misgivings. He planted his lips on mine and slipped his tongue in my mouth. I placed my hands on his chest, leaning into him. I didn't want the kissing to end, but when it did, I was pleased to see Zeke and Claire making out too. Claire and I smiled at each other, embarrassed.

"I want to get you a present," Joey said suddenly, smiling mischievously. He led the way back into the mall, and directed us toward a small jewelry boutique that sold trendy costume jewelry, hair accessories, and handbags. Was Joey actually going to buy me a piece of jewelry? If so, did that mean we were dating?

My mixed emotions and scattered thoughts induced by the pot made me nervous and overly introspective. "Wait for us at those benches across from the store," Zeke instructed, pointing to a narrow set of empty seats. *Was this just an excuse to get rid of us? What was going on?* I wondered, my thoughts spinning ceaselessly in meaningless, paranoid circles. The pot was making my thoughts seem strange, as though they weren't my own.

Nevertheless, Claire and I sat there waiting, straining our eyes to see what the boys were doing exactly. Nearly half an hour later, they came walking out of the boutique, without bags. "Let's go for a smoke," Joey suggested.

I shook my head. "I can't smoke anymore of that

stuff. My head is already all messed up…"

"Not that, silly. Let's go have a cigarette. You do smoke cigarettes, don't you?" he asked, poking at me playfully. "From time to time," I answered coyly, which was a total lie. I'd never smoked a cigarette in my life.

We headed back out to the front of the plaza, but we didn't hide this time. We stood right in front of the mall, where cars were parked along the emergency lane, parents picking up their kids. Zeke and Joey lit up their cigarettes. They offered me one, but this time I declined. It was nearing 10:30, and I couldn't take the risk of Claire's mom pulling up early and catching us smoking.

"We need to get going in a few minutes. We have to meet back up with my sister before we go wait for our ride home," Claire said. She looked irritated. I think she was still sore about not getting a present from the boutique as promised. Right on cue, the boys handed us each a matching set of necklaces and earrings.

The necklace was a flimsy chain, but it contained a gorgeous silver heart in its center that opened up to reveal a tiny space for a picture. The heart had three words engraved on its front: *I Love You.* I couldn't believe it.

My hands were shaking as I accepted his gift, and I glanced at Claire's reaction to her own jewelry. She was grinning from ear to ear. The earrings were also quite nice, two tiny cubic zirconia "diamonds." I couldn't help myself; I reached out for Joey, throwing my arms around his neck gleefully.

But before I could even say "thank you" for the gift, I heard sounds of shouting from behind us. "Stop right there!" yelled a grey-headed, overweight security guard. He was running right toward us. A petite, impeccably dressed sales associate, who I recognized from the boutique, was jogging right beside him.

"That's them! The ones who were shoplifting!" she declared, pointing an accusatory finger in our direction. As the security guard came running, Zeke and Joey took off across the plaza parking lot, leaving Claire and I stranded with the stolen merchandise in our hands.

Chapter Two

I know I should have been pissed at Joey, but I can honestly say that I wasn't. I knew he genuinely liked me and stole the jewelry because he couldn't afford to buy it on his own. You remember that old saying, 'It's the thought that counts'? Shouldn't that apply in this situation?

Needless to say, I still liked Joey. But my feelings didn't matter anymore because I was grounded for a month. No trips to the mall and no phone. It could have been worse, my mom said: they could have taken us to jail. Instead, they held Claire and I in a cramped security office until Claire's mom came to pick us up. When she arrived, they told her we were involved in a shoplifting scheme with two boys. To make matters worse, Claire's mom told my mom everything, of course.

Not only was I grounded for a month, my mom informed me that I would no longer be allowed to go the mall without her until I was at least sixteen. I never expected to see Joey again. I would just have to learn to deal with it.

I spent that month in my room, sneaking cigarettes from my mother any chance I got. At night, while my parents slept, I would climb out my window and sit on the roof, enjoying the rich, minty flavor of my mother's Newports. I wrote sappy love poems for Joey, poems he would never have a chance to read. I flipped through radio channels compulsively, searching for either the angriest or the saddest songs I could find. I felt depressed, simple as that.

Around the time my month-long grounding came to an end, school went back in session. I was eager for the first day because it meant I could leave the house. Most importantly, it meant I would get to see my best friend again. Claire and I hadn't talked since that night at the plaza.

She was waiting for me at the front entrance of school when I walked through the door lined with metal detectors. In a small town like this, you would think there'd be no need for such extreme measures, but the truth is, school was just as dangerous, if not more dangerous, than a plaza filled with strangers. I just wished my mother understood that.

I smiled at Claire. She was dressed in a trendy pair of overalls, and she was wearing them the way cool kids do, with one strap left undone. She had chin-length brown hair with a button nose and freckles. She was definitely what most boys would consider 'cute.' I, on the other hand, did not feel cute, or pretty for that matter. Not with my long black hair, dark eyes, and curvy bottom that didn't match my flat chest. Lately, I'd been experimenting with makeup, and today I was wearing maroon-colored lipstick and black eyeliner drawn so far off my eyes that I looked Egyptian.

The first words out of Claire's mouth were, "I have a plan." I immediately knew she was talking about something that had to do with Joey and Zeke. Claire and I had been best friends since kindergarten and sometimes we could communicate with just a few simple words. She was definitely up to something.

I looked at her questioningly. She handed me a party invitation, one of those simple kinds that you buy at the store and fill out by hand on your own. The first line said 'Party For' and in the blank beside it was a handwritten name:

Denver Reynolds

Denver Reynolds was a girl in our same grade, a mutual friend of ours that we'd hung out with in the past. She was rather stuck up, so we didn't spend time with her too often. She was one of those girls whose mother always showed up for parent-teacher meetings and bought her the latest, trendiest clothes and accessories. I shrugged my shoulders. "So?" I asked, irritated.

"So, look where the party is," Claire whined impatiently. My eyes scanned the list, passing by 'Time' and 'Date.' The bottom blank was for 'Place' and it read in loopy, cursive writing:

The Riverside Roller Rink

I still didn't see the big deal, and I told Claire so.

"The big deal," she said, "is that there is no party at the Riverside Roller Rink."

"Huh?" I said, baffled by her secretive tone. "My mom ungrounded me last week. So, I was able to finally call Zeke. He asked me to give him the name of a girl from my school, and he told me that he would send us an invitation to hang out with him and Joey, only he sent it under the name of our good old classmate and friend, Denver Reynolds," she explained. "It's brilliant, right?"

I stopped walking down the hallway, and glared at my friend, stunned. "Are you telling me that we're supposed to meet Joey and Zeke at the roller skating rink this Saturday?" I asked incredulously. "Yes!" she squealed, clapping her hands together gaily.

I shushed her, looking around to make sure no one was listening. As much as I wanted to see Joey, this whole thing sounded pretty risky. If my mom found out I was lying to her again, I would be grounded until I turned eighteen. Not to mention the fact that I was supposed to be grounded until next Monday. I told Claire the unfortunate news about the length of my most recent punishment.

"Oh, Wendi! You know your mom will let you attend a party if it's for one of your classmates. Especially since she knows that Denver's parents will be at the party."

"But that's the thing...there won't be any parents, and there is no party, Claire! Do you really think we should do this?" I asked worriedly.

The look she gave me was one I'd never seen

before from Claire. It was a hateful, disgusted sneer that didn't seem to fit with her cutesy, freckly face. She said, "I'm going with or without you, so make up your mind," and then she stomped haughtily off down the hallway.

Chapter Three

My mother pulled up to the front of the boxy brick building that was the Riverside Roller Rink. "I want you to understand that the only reason I'm letting you go, even though you're grounded, is because I want to give you a chance to make some new friends. Denver Reynolds is a nice, studious girl," my mother said approvingly. She didn't have to say it, but I knew she meant to add, "Unlike Claire."

"I'll pick you up at eleven o'clock. Be waiting out front for me. If you have any problems, call me on my beeper or cell. And Wendi? There had better be no problems tonight like there was last time..." she said, shooting me a warning glance.

"I'll be good, Mom. I promise," I lied, leaning over to kiss her on the cheek. Despite my recent grounding and her overprotective nature, I truly loved and respected my mother. I hated lying to her.

Handing me a twenty dollar bill, she reminded me to grab Denver's present from the backseat. I knew I'd look like a total doofus carrying a present for a party that I wasn't even attending. But I had to keep up appearances, so I pulled the heavy, perfectly wrapped box out from the backseat, and then I waved goodbye to my mom.

I pulled open the heavy metal doors to the skating rink. Right away, I was hit by the outrageously loud sounds and vibrations from the music inside. I paid the five dollar entry fee to an elderly, frowning man at the front, and I went through another door into the rink.

The place was jet-black and the music so loud that I was initially disoriented. The rink in the middle was the only well-lit section in the building, but the vivid, flashing strobe lights just made everything around me that much more hectic and confusing. The dark space was filled with clouds of cigarette smoke, with kids my age lighting up everywhere. I'd come here once with a few of my cousins when I was little, and it certainly didn't look like this then. I'd been under the assumption that skating rinks were family-oriented; that was not the case with Riverside.

The place was packed full of moving bodies; there were some families, but mostly teenagers. The center area was filled with people on skates. Some of the smaller children hugged the outer rails while the older kids zoomed by, crossing their legs in a zigzag motion, doing some sort of version of hip-hop dancing on skates. I didn't remember how to skate, and I was suddenly filled with a sense of dread. I had no idea where Claire or the boys were, and it was too crowded to see anyone or anything around me.

Even if I wanted to shout out Claire's name, it wouldn't have helped because of the booming sounds of the music and people's voices buzzing on all sides of me. I waded through the crowds, saying "Excuse me" at least a dozen times. It didn't help that I was carrying the big, bulky present in my arms.

Up ahead, I spotted several rows of table booths, and noticed a couple of them were empty. Finally picking one, I sat down with relief. I rested the gift in the center of the table, spinning it around in circles anxiously. At least from here I could look around the entire rink and try to find Claire or one of the boys. A group of teenagers in a nearby booth were staring at me, and I tried my best to avoid their eyes. I felt like an idiot sitting there by myself with the babyish present in front of me.

After nearly ten minutes of looking around awkwardly, I felt a soft push on my shoulder from behind. Startled, I turned around in my seat to find Claire, Joey, and Zeke smiling down at me. Up until now, I'd been irritated. But looking at Joey made my heart melt. I unconsciously fingered the locket on my neck. I was happy to see him, and relieved to no longer be on my own.

"Let's get out of here!" Claire shouted over the music. "But I just paid to get in!" I hollered back. She shrugged. "Joey and Zeke live a couple blocks from here. We're gonna hang out at their house."

I gave her a look, letting her know I wasn't crazy about the idea. I thought about that girl I saw earlier today at school, the one who seemed very different from my childhood best friend. But it was my friend who leaned down and whispered, "Don't worry, Wendi. Joey's mom and stepdad are going to be there. I promise, if it's weird, just give me a look and we'll get out of there pronto. I got your back, girl."

"What am I supposed to do with this present?" I asked, staring down at its girlish wrapping paper and glittery ribbon. For the first time, I wondered what was inside the stupid thing. "I'll carry it for you," Joey offered, picking it up from the table. "Okay," I said, standing up to leave. I trailed behind the three of them and left into the night.

The streets behind the skating rink were shrouded in darkness, and the houses that lined them seemed unoccupied. I'd never been through this subdivision before, and I had to admit it seemed sort of rundown. Many of the houses had boarded up windows and porches filled with unused clutter and appliances. We had only gone a couple blocks when I noticed a pair of headlights up ahead at the end of the street. A vehicle was headed straight for us.

As it approached, I realized it was a stretch limousine, but not one of those fancy ones. This one had faded paint and dents along its fender. The surprising thing wasn't the limo's pitiful appearance, but the fact that it actually seemed to be stopping beside us. The driver screeched to a halt and I nearly jumped out of my own skin.

"A fancy ride for a fancy lady," Joey whispered in my ear, giving me a comforting squeeze. "You know the driver?" I asked, looking up at him, baffled. "My stepdad," he said, just as the limo driver rolled down his window. A cloud of smoke flowed out from it. A ruddy faced, gap-toothed man looked out at us.

"Want to go for a ride?" he asked, smiling at us creepily. If he wasn't Joey's stepfather, I'd have told this weirdo to go fuck himself. Zeke did the honors of opening the door to the back for us. Claire climbed in first and I followed reluctantly behind her.

Joey and Zeke got in, and the four of us sat side by side on the dingy bench seat of the limo. It was riddled with dark stains and cigarette burns. Not only that, but it smelled. I shuddered involuntarily. I couldn't help feeling creeped out. I'm not sure what I'd expected of this evening, but riding around this dark town in a crummy limousine with a creepy old man certainly wasn't on my agenda.

"Where are we going?" I asked fearfully.

"My stepdad is picking up a client and then he's going to take us back to the house. We can hang out there for a bit, and then I'll have him take you guys back before your mom gets back," Joey reassured. He slipped his hand in mine, stroking the back of my hand with his fingers soothingly.

That damn present sat at our feet and we rode along in silence. Soft music was playing, something jazzy and foreign to me. Suddenly, the tinted driver's window slid down, and his stepdad smiled back at us in the rearview mirror. "You kids want a joint?" he asked, taking one hand from the wheel and using it to dig around in the console beside him.

Joey got up and went to the window, taking the pot from his stepdad. The thought of a parent offering us drugs was hard for me to fathom, but I suppose, in a way, it was cool. Joey sat back down, lighting the joint and handing it to me. I took one small toke, hesitant to get too high and lose my wits again. I was still unsure about this situation. The last thing I wanted to do was get in trouble with my parents again, and I had a sinking feeling that was exactly where this evening was headed.

I was surprised to see Claire looking calm and relaxed as she took long drags from the joint. Zeke was stroking one of her arms, his eyes focused on her intently. Joey stared at me too, but I kept my eyes straight ahead. I kept imagining what my mother and father were doing; they were probably watching TV and relaxing, completely unaware of the trouble I was getting myself into.

Several minutes later, our driver parked on the street in front of a two-story, cape cod-styled house. It was made of brick, with steep, crumbling stairs leading up to its roomy front porch. Joey's stepdad got out from the driver's seat and closed the heavy limo door behind him. I wiggled around in my seat uncomfortably, my butt sticking to its dirty fabric, wondering again who it was we were picking up. I jumped as our door flew open and Joey's stepdad stuck his head in.

He said, "Come in and say hi to Aunt Jeanna."

"Okay." Joey let out a whoosh of breath. "Come in with me," Joey said, looking at all three of us expectantly. Zeke and Claire followed Joey out of the limo, so I had no choice but to go. I got out warily, running fingers through my long, tangled hair. Slowly, I ascended the dark stairs and stood on the porch while Joey's stepdad knocked.

There were several lights on inside, and the door was answered instantly by a gorgeous blonde who didn't look a day over thirty. "About time!" she exclaimed, walking into the front living room and leaving the door wide open for us.

I brought up the rear as we all entered the home one after the other. By the time we all filed in, Joey's Aunt Jeanna was sitting on a worn leather armchair with her legs tucked beneath her, a sour look on her face. Joey's stepdad, who she referred to as Jed, took a seat on the flowery sectional beside her chair.

Claire and Zeke sat down beside him, leaving one empty space. I half expected Joey to plop down in it, leaving me with nowhere to sit, but he motioned for me to take it. I sat down, placing my hands in my lap awkwardly.

"Well, where's my shit?" Jeanna demanded rudely, looking straight at Jed. He reached in his coat pocket, retrieving a Ziploc bag filled with yellowish white chunks of crystal-like matter. He tossed it in her lap and leaned back against the couch cushions, folding his fingers over his bulbous belly. Jeanna looked at the bag, a smile forming at the corners of her mouth.

"And the rest of it?" she asked, glancing up at me and Claire. She looked from one of us to the other. *Was she talking to me?* I wondered nervously. What could I possibly have that she wants?

"Yep," Jed answered dryly. She looked away from me and back at him. "Great," she said, digging one of the bigger chunks out of the bag. This whole situation felt weird to me, and I wanted to get out of here more than any other place I'd been to in my life. It was my understanding that Jed was picking up a client, not dropping off drugs to Joey's crazy aunt. I shifted in the seat uncomfortably, watching Jeanna drop bits of the drug into a skinny glass pipe with an odd-shaped bowl on its end. She held a lighter to the end of it, taking long puffs as she stared at the tip. She didn't offer us any, for which I was grateful. I wasn't exactly sure what she was smoking, but I had a few ideas.

We sat there, watching her smoke and listening to the dull sounds of a radio playing in the kitchen. After a while, I couldn't sit still any longer. I picked at the hangnails on my thumbs until I could pick no longer.

"I need to go back," I whispered to Joey. He nodded.

"Jed, I have to get my friends back soon," Joey announced, still standing up with his arms crossed over his chest. He truly was adorable, with his bronze-colored skin and baby fine, almost white hair.

"Okey dokey," Jed replied, getting up from the couch. He, Joey, and Zeke said their goodbyes, and we headed back out to the limo. Jeanna was still puffing away desperately as I went through the door. I was relieved to be back outside in the damp, cool air.

"I need to get back to the skating rink. I can't afford to get grounded again," I said as soon as we were seated in the back.

"We're going to my house now," Joey said. "I promise I'll make sure you're back to the skating rink in plenty of time," he added, a whining tone to his voice.

"No," I answered firmly. "I need to go back now. If you want to hang out with me, then you can do it at the skating rink. And if your stepdad won't take me, then just drop me off and I'll walk back from here."

Claire was staring at me with a dirty, mocking look on her face. I gave her an ugly look in return. Screw Claire. If she wanted to choose Zeke over me, then so be it. I didn't feel comfortable and I wanted to go back. I was sticking to my guns this time.

"Okay. We'll take you back," Joey offered sweetly. He tapped on the tinted driver's window and whispered to his stepdad in a hushed tone.

"We'll take you now," Jed said, looking back in the mirror at me. His eyes stayed on mine for a minute too long, and my stomach fluttered nervously.

We rode back in silence again. They passed the joint back and forth, but I held up a hand to decline. The next thing I knew, they were pulling up in front of the skating rink. The limo pulled off and I was left standing alone in the parking lot, holding Denver Reynolds' phony birthday present again.

I jogged across the lot, heading back to the entrance. The front of the rink was deserted, and so was the parking lot. I pulled on the doors, but was surprised to discover they were locked. I glanced down at my watch. It was 10:18. The party invitation had read eight until eleven. But then again, the invitation had been a fake.

I looked at the sign on the door. The roller skating rink had closed at 9:30. "Well, isn't this just great," I muttered miserably. So, here I was, stuck waiting in the dark, alone. The only thing I had to keep me company was the present at my feet. I suddenly realized I was going to have to lose the present before my mom showed up. How would I explain the fact that I still had it after going to a birthday party? I looked around anxiously, wondering if I should perhaps toss it in the bushes.

I considered calling my mother, but then she would know it had all been a lie. I simply couldn't risk it. I had no other choice but to sit and wait. She would be here in forty minutes. I sat on the front stoop miserably. I still had the present, unsure what to do with it. *I'm just going to tell her the truth*, I decided unexpectedly. I'll tell her that I screwed up and tell her I was scared. Maybe it would feel good talking to someone about it. About everything.

Minutes dragged by lazily, the night air cool, with one sole street lamp providing me comfort. I was nearly half asleep with my head in my hands when I heard the sounds of a car approaching. I immediately saw a dark Chevy blazer, definitely not my mother's car. It pulled into the parking lot, which caught me by surprise. I stood up and stepped back as the driver pulled up right in front of the rink.

Suddenly, the passenger door to the Blazer flew open and a surly looking man got out. Before I even had a chance to stand up, he grabbed me around the waist and lifted me off the ground. I kicked and screamed angrily, clawing at his eyes and skin. He threw me in the backseat. My body hit the cold, vinyl surface of the seat, and I let out an *oomph* sound.

I felt slightly dazed, and when I looked up, I was stunned to see Joey's crazy Aunt Jeanna seated up front in the passenger seat. She smiled back at me maniacally, and then the driver got in his seat, and pulled off hastily. I was in complete and utter shock, still trying to wrap my brain around what was happening. I mean, you hear about this stuff in the movies, but in real life? It didn't seem logical. Why would these strange people kidnap me? *Maybe they are playing some sort of prank*, I considered. But that premise seemed unlikely. My chest filled with dread.

I wouldn't swear to it, but as we drove away I thought we passed my mom's Kia pulling in the lot. I beat my palms against the back window, slamming them against the glass, letting out a deep, guttural scream. If only my mother had gotten there a few minutes earlier. *Now I was never going to see her again*, I realized fearfully. Pounding on the glass, I watched the rink drift farther and farther away from view.

Suddenly, the glass window was covered in some sort of liquid, all sticky and red. I stared at it incredulously, realizing that I'd beaten my hands so hard they were raw and bleeding.

I didn't care about the blood, or the state of my hands. Turning toward my captors, I was ready to make *them* bleed…but then the driver reached back, holding something in his hand…and then my head exploded with a sharp pain. My whole world went black.

***

I awoke in a black, dank room. Here's what I could see—nothing. Lying on my back, I realized my hands and feet were restrained. A shrill, piercing sound reverberated in my head. Eventually, I realized it was the sounds of my own screaming. Like the blood, my body was releasing strange sounds and substances, and nothing about this situation made sense.

My head felt heavy and painful, and for a moment, I wondered if I'd been shot in the skull. *No, silly…If you'd been shot in the head, then you'd be dead by now*, I chastised myself. They must have hit me over the head with something heavy, something sturdy enough to knock me unconscious.

I tried to look around, struggling to sharpen my focus in the dark. But still, there was nothing, and all I could do was scream and pray that someone, somewhere, could possibly hear me.

My captors reacted to my screams strangely; they turned up the volume on the music that played outside of the room. A haunting voice sang about the end, how his only friend was the end…

Something about the song was familiar, but yet it seemed foreign to me somehow too. I laid there in the darkness, listening to those lyrics, my eyes widened in fright. When the song finally ended, it began again, an endless tune on repeat. Jerking my head and body from side to side, I tried to loosen my restraints. After a while, I started to wonder if the song was still playing in reality, or if it was all in my head.

I began to hyperventilate, struggling against the shackles that engulfed my wrists and ankles. With the tips of my fingers, I'd discovered my restraints were metal, so there was no breaking free from them.

I'm going to die, I realized. I screamed some more until my throat felt as though it were filled with fire and a dozen tiny needles. I thought about water and ice. *And everything nice*, I thought strangely, delirious from my concussion and overwhelming terror. I started banging my head against the floor beneath me; I'm still unsure what I was trying to accomplish. Eventually, I either went unconscious or fell into a deep sleep. I dreamt of snakes, the lyrics of that song playing over and over again in my head, even in my sleep.

Chapter Four

I woke to the sounds of birds chirping. Without opening my eyes, I sniffed at the air, praying that since it was Sunday, my mom would be making her world famous pancakes. She would add a handful of blackberries or strawberries to the batter, and they always tasted so good and fresh in the mornings. But then my thoughts shifted, and I remembered the dark Blazer and the pounding music that'd filled that hellish room.

I opened my eyes slowly. I was no longer restrained, but I was in a room that unfortunately, was not my girlishly decorated room in Flocksdale. I was on a thinly carpeted floor in a small, ten by twelve room. Most likely the same room I'd been in last night. The room was lacking furniture and anything, really, except for me and...I looked behind me, only to discover a woman sitting at a glass-topped vanity table, her back facing toward me.

The woman was wearing a sheer bra and panties, with a sweeping mane of long blonde hair that trailed down past her bra line. The face in the mirror was Jeanna's. Her reflected eyes met mine, and she whirled around in her velvety seat to face me. Her eyes were colorless and frightening.

My wrists and ankles were covered in bruises and bloody sores. My head felt like a steel ball, the weight of it crushing down on my stiff shoulders. I rubbed at my wrists, then gently touched the wound on top of my head, all the while glaring into Jeanna's beady little eyes. I was going to kill this junkie bitch the first chance I had.

"Take me home," I croaked, my throat raw from last night's screaming session. I barely recognized the sound of my own voice.

"I can't do that," she said calmly, whipping back around to face the mirror. Gracefully, she lifted a wand of mascara, brushing it lightly over her lashes. After that, she set to work curling her lashes with one of those strange metal contraptions that only serious makeup-users own. Sitting up, I tucked my knees to my chest. She continued to act as though I wasn't there.

"Why am I here? I don't even know you! I haven't done anything to deserve being tortured!" I screamed, rising painfully to my feet. I clenched my hands into angry fists. *I could go after her right now*, I thought angrily. But if Jeanna considered the idea of me attacking her, she didn't seem concerned. She stared straight ahead, concentrating on her beauty routine.

After a long time, she spoke. "To answer your question, you haven't done anything wrong but just be you, darlin'." Now she was using an eyebrow pencil to darken her brows. "A lot of men will pay a lot of money to be with a young girl like you. Garrett's got some men lined up for you tonight."

My eyes widened, my body rigid with fear.

"Don't look so scared, honey. I'll give you something for the pain," she offered, tapping a finger on the vanity's glass top, which contained a skinny line of a powdery, brownish substance.

"I don't do drugs, you bitch!" I screamed, suddenly hit with a rush of overwhelming anger. I ran toward her with a surge of fearless adrenaline, my body crashing into hers. I grabbed a fistful of hair and tried to dig my nails into her scalp.

Suddenly she was on her feet and the next thing I knew, she was sprawled out on top of me, pinning my arms at my sides. She smiled down at me, a small trickle of blood dripping from her lip. I didn't remember hitting her face, but I was glad to have caused some damage. A droplet of her blood hit the tip of my nose. I jerked back from her in disgust. Gripping my wrists forcefully, she used her weight to restrain the lower half of my body. "Do that again and I'll kill ya. Better yet, I'll sell you into permanent slavery," she warned.

I stopped struggling and looked at her crazily. "Kill me then," I challenged bitterly, giving her a crazy, wide-eyed stare. "I would rather be dead than do what you want me to do!"

"That's what Claire said too," Jeanna whispered softly, releasing my arms to wipe her bloody lip.

I lay there, frozen. My heart stopped momentarily and the room seemed devoid of any air. She couldn't be telling the truth...why would she mention Claire? Suddenly, the whole room was spinning.

When I last saw Claire, she was headed in the other direction with Joey and Zeke in the limousine. Joey and Zeke...their stepdad introduced us to Jeanna...Oh, no! I realized then that I wasn't the only one in danger. They must have taken Claire too!

I thought about that ride in the limo and going to Jeanna's house. She was acting so strangely, but I didn't understand it, and then something clicked. When Jeanna asked about her "stuff," she must have been referring to me and Claire!

"It was all a setup, wasn't it? Joey and Zeke didn't like us. They recruited us for you, their *aunt*," I said softly. Jeanna didn't answer. She stood up, dusting nonexistent debris from her bare legs.

She walked out of the room, gently closing the bedroom door behind her, leaving me alone again. It was a terrifying feeling, but at least this time I wasn't strapped down or in the dark.

Chapter Five

I spent most of the late afternoon being dolled up by Jeanna. She told some crazy story about being sold into the sex slave business at a young age. I didn't know if I believed her. "Now I'm a part-owner of the business," she announced proudly, raising her eyebrows at me.

"Do you want a fucking cookie?" I spat angrily.

My anger didn't faze her. Jeanna was tough and shrewd, cold as winter and hard as ice. Nothing I said seemed to break through her calm, sociopathic demeanor. She kept working on my hair, humming a melancholic tune I didn't recognize.

"Where is Claire?" I demanded for the twentieth time, emphasizing each word slowly and angrily.

"I don't know," Jeanna admitted, setting down the brush and shrugging her shoulders casually. "She went with Garrett to a separate set of buyers. Like I told you before, we don't keep girls long term. You're no good to us all used up," she explained calmly, twisting my hair painfully with the curling iron.

Jeanna had a gun tucked in the back of her jeans. I'd seen it earlier, as she'd moved around the room. If I was strong enough to wrestle her for it, and knew how to fire a gun, I would go for it. Finished with my hair, she started applying gobs of makeup to my face. Thick powder and creams. My eyes glazed over, focused on thoughts of the gun, imagining myself holding its shiny, steel body in my hand. Watching her concealer-caked face blow apart as I pulled the trigger, and giving no sense of hesitation…

I opened my eyes; the girl in the mirror staring back at me looked like a circus clown, with heavy rouge and thick gobs of black, spidery mascara on her lashes. "I don't get it. If these creeps want to fuck a child, then why the fuck are you making me look like a full grown woman?" I asked, whipping around in my chair to face her.

She paused, mulling over my question. "They don't want to fuck children. They want to fuck innocent young women. You're the closest thing," she muttered softly.

"So, you really think I believe you when you say you're going to let me go? I may be young, but I'm not a moron." She started lining my eyes with heavy eye shadow and liner, to match the big lashes below.

"Like I said, Wendi, I have no use for you. If I kill you, then that would leave evidence. If I let you go, there will be none." She applied another coat of powder around my eyes, the edges of the makeup pad slicing the bottom of my eyelids painfully.

I looked at her like she was crazy. *She is crazy*, I

realized. "*I'm* the evidence, dead or alive. They will still track you down," I threatened.

Again, she smiled. She sat down on a stool across from where I was perched on my own. "You don't know our real names, honey. You don't know where you are. They'll never find us, Wendi," she stated matter-of-factly.

"I know where you live. Remember how Jed brought your drugs to the house? I was with him, you idiot," I reminded her. She abruptly smacked me across the face, knocking me off the seat sideways. I sat there on my knees, catching my breath, my hand covering the spot she'd battered on my face. The angry blow was shocking compared to her statuesque demeanor. I tried to rub the stinging sensation away.

"His name isn't Jed. Joey and Zeke, also not their names, are not even related to *Jed*. He doesn't really drive a limo. And that house you met me at? Also a set up. That is not where I live, *you* idiot," she retorted.

I was dumbfounded. She dropped her powder brush and walked out of the room, leaving me there on my knees by the vanity table. I pulled myself up to my feet, my body still shaking. I sat at the vanity table for hours, dozing for a short while, my curly hair and made up face splayed out across the table.

There were two small windows in the room, but they were too high and minuscule to do me any good. The door was locked, obviously. The only thing in the room besides my previously used shackles and the vanity table was a narrow antique-looking vent on the floor in the farthest left hand corner. When I woke up from napping, I headed straight for it, a newfound energy in my step.

Lying on the floor, I fiddled with a small metal switch attached to the slatted vents. I pulled it down hard and suddenly, it was open, and I could see the contours of a room below. Wherever I was, I was upstairs, because I could see a small bedroom displayed beneath me.

I wasn't ready to scream down into the vent just yet, fearful of attracting the attention of Jeanna, or someone inherently worse. I pressed my face against the vent, scoping out the room below. Like my room, it was mostly empty. There was a free-standing bookshelf, but that was all I could see. Then suddenly, a flash of something moved past the vent. I jumped back, startled. But then I crawled back over, hesitantly looking back through the slats, holding my breath as I peered down below. I let out a cry of relief. It was Claire!

Chapter Six

"Claire?" I whispered down through the grate. Tears were streaming down my face, my body trembling with distress. Finding my friend was bittersweet; I didn't want her to be here with me, but seeing her meant she was still alive. I felt a mixture of emotions rushing through me: relief, sadness, and then anger. How could they do this to us? What sort of sick, depraved individual would kidnap two young girls? And then, most importantly: how the hell were we going to get out of this situation?

Claire looked around the room, confused. I whispered down to her again. When she looked up and met my gaze, she let out a small cry of dismay. I put a finger to my lips, shushing her.

She started moving around, and I couldn't help wondering what she was up to. But then I understood as I saw her shoving the bookshelf across the room, lining it up directly under the vent. She climbed it slowly, treating the shelves like steps on a ladder so she could get closer. When she was standing on top of it, she stuck her long fingers up through the slats, intertwining them with mine.

I wept uncontrollably, gripping her fingers as tightly as possible. Claire always had a silver ring on her thumb, and her arms were encircled with nearly a dozen macramé bracelets, the kind you can spell out words with in tiny beads. I stared at the tiny letters, still unsure what they all spelled, my eyes brimming over with tears.

"What happened to you?" I asked hesitantly. It sounded like a stupid question. Did it really matter how we got here anymore? All that mattered now was that we were here in captivity, and finding a way out was imperative. Now I had to figure out how to get myself *and* my best friend out of here. *Damn them for doing this to us!*

"Joey and Zeke…it was all a trick, Wendi! They held me down and tied me up. They blindfolded me and brought me to this room…" Claire explained, holding her head down to her chest, shamefully. "I kicked and screamed, but there was nothing I could do! They were just too strong." She let out a whimper.

I shook my head woefully.

"How did they get you?" she asked, searching my eyes. Briefly, I described how I was kidnapped from the skating rink by Jeanna and a man she called Garrett. Claire looked at me, her face consumed with guilt and sadness. "I'm so sorry, Wendi. This is my fault…I should have listened, and I never should have followed those boys…I'm so freaking stupid…"

I shushed her again. "You most certainly aren't, and it's just as much my fault as yours," I tried to reassure her. "Are there windows in there?" I asked hopefully, trying to scope out as much of the space below as possible. "Yeah, but the windows are covered in metal bars," she said, squinting up at me.

"What is out there? Can you see through the bars?" I asked, suddenly feeling hopeful. She shook her head dejectedly. "It's blacked out. It looks like the outside of the windows are covered in thick wooden boards, or something."

I leaned my back against the wall, feeling rueful and helpless. I was tempted to tear at my own hair and clothes, screaming until they were forced to kill me. If the walls were barred on the inside and boarded up on the outside, there was definitely no way to escape through the windows. The windows at the top of my room were too small and too high to do me any good. There was nothing for me to climb on to reach them, and even if there was, they were too small and high to climb through. My thoughts were racing; my blood was pumping. I'd always been the sort of person who just figured shit out, the leader of the group, but I was at a loss right now...

But then it occurred to me—the only way out was through the doors to the rooms we were concealed in. I had to overtake Jeanna, or whoever came through those doors next. But I had no weapons. Pacing around the room excitedly, I tried to come up with something, anything... "Is there anything you can use as a weapon down there?" I asked, squatting back down by the grate. Claire

43

shook her head dejectedly.

All this speculation was useless. Claire and I were going to die if we didn't figure out something soon.

Chapter Seven

Even though this situation seemed hopeless, I couldn't give up yet. I had to get me and my best friend out of this mess. *Or die trying*, I thought miserably. "We have to fight back, Claire. If we don't, we're going to die," I told her solemnly.

"But she said she would let us go."

"Who? Jeanna? She's a lying bitch, Claire! She's not going to let us go. She—or that man of hers, the one she calls Garrett—will kill both of us. We can't trust a word they say."

Claire nodded grimly, seemingly accepting my words as truth.

"Whenever she comes back, we must attack with all of our might," I instructed. Claire nodded again. She stepped down from the bookshelf, moving it back in place as quietly as possible.

I sat glumly with my back against the wall, waiting for Jeanna to return, but she never did. I listened for footsteps or voices through the door, but heard nothing. I eventually scooted back over to the vent, comforted by the thought of my best friend

45

being so close, even though she was technically out of reach. I wrapped my arms around my knees, waiting patiently. I tried to refrain from humming that dreadful song…the one about the end…

Suddenly, there were scuffling sounds coming up through the open vent. I stuck my face to the grate again, peering down anxiously. I saw Claire wrestling with a woman, but it wasn't Jeanna. This woman was smaller and stouter, probably one of Jeanna's helpers.

Claire screamed shrilly, clawing at the woman's face and hands, trying to overtake her. The woman was on top of her now. "Hey—up here, bitch!" I screamed. My shouting distracted her; she looked up toward the ceiling, and when she did, Claire coldcocked her in the jaw. The woman fell to the ground hard, hitting heavily like a dumpy sack of potatoes.

"Run, Claire! Run through the door!" I screamed, my heart lurching with excitement and fear. I was pounding my fists against the grates, rooting for my best friend. "Go, go, go, go, go!"

Claire ran for the door. She swung it open and went through. I couldn't see her anymore, but I could see the fallen woman on the floor. She was getting up.

"Run, Claire, run! She's awake!" I screamed. The woman jumped up, shot an evil look up at me, and went charging through the door behind Claire. I could see and hear nothing for several moments. I closed my eyes and murmured *The Lord's Prayer* over and over again. My grandmother taught it to me when I was little, and I couldn't believe I was still able to recall the chant. "Give us this day, our daily bread…And forgive us our trespasses…As we forgive those who trespass against us…"

I was still repeating the prayer when several moments later I heard the door to the room below opening. I squinted down through the grate, trying to see what was happening. Again it was the stout woman. She was bent over in the door frame, with her wide rear end pointed in my direction. She moved backwards, dragging something across the floor.

I gasped, jumping back from the grated vent. She was pulling my best friend's body across the floor.

Chapter Eight

Claire was dead and it was my fault. Her face, with all of its adorable features, was smashed in, making her barely recognizable. Her dull, open eyes stared up at me lifelessly. I sunk to the floor and crawled away from the image below.

I didn't cry. I just sat there, sucking in shallow, raspy breaths of air. Edging back over, I looked through it again. Once more I was met with the image of Claire's lifeless eyes and broken face. It was hard to believe that only moments ago she was looking up here, an animated human form. I shuddered, overwhelmed with grief and hatred for my captors.

Claire was dead. "You're next," I imagined a voice saying in my head. I clamped my hands over my ears, begging the voice to stop. I rocked back and forth, keeping my ears covered...*They killed my friend. She's dead. She's gone. And crying won't help me.*

I jumped to my feet, charging toward the locked door in front of me, punching with all my might, screaming at the top of my lungs. I kicked at the door angrily, cracking the wood with my foot. "Come fight me, bitch!" I screamed, kicking more forcefully at the splintered wood.

Suddenly, the door flew open and Jeanna came charging in. I swung a punch in her direction, but she charged toward my middle, knocking me to the floor. The back of my head slammed against the hard floor beneath me, sending vibrations of pain throughout my entire body. She had me pinned, but I fought and kicked at her ceaselessly, howling and growling wildly.

A needle emerged from her jeans pocket. I watched helplessly as she jabbed it into my forearm. "No, no, no, no..." I pleaded, but then I was hit with a wave of something cool and calm. My body became soft and pliable. I slept dreamlessly.

Chapter Nine

Despite my earlier protests, I became grateful for the drugs. I spent the next...hours? Days? Weeks...lying on my back in that dingy, dilapidated house, the faces of men hovering over me. The smell of their breath and body fluids were putrid.

The drugs kept me numb and sedated. Jeanna kept me fed and brought me water often. A few times she lifted me into the bathtub and washed me, as I was too weak to perform the simple task myself.

I felt nothing except the loss of my friend. The image of her face, with her dead eyes so empty and cold, swarmed through my mind, presenting itself over and over like an endless loop. Claire was dead and gone, and nothing I could say or do would ever bring her back. When I closed my eyes, I thought about her bracelet and those tiny little beads.

One night, while I was nodding out from the heroin, I dreamt I was in my old bedroom at my parents' house. The carpet of my room was covered from one end to the other with tiny lettered beads, and they rose higher and higher, edging their way to the popcorn-patterned ceiling above. I jerked my arms out in front of me flimsily, a lame attempt at swimming through a sea of substance that in no way resembled water. Eventually, my face and head were covered with the hard little beads, and they filled my mouth and throat. I couldn't breathe, and all I could think was that if I could just figure out what all the lettered beads spelled, I would somehow be saved from drowning in them.

I also dreamt of Claire's face, and the faceless men that surrounded me in the darkness of that horrible room. Jeanna kept me so heavily drugged that I didn't know when I was dreaming and when I wasn't, honestly.

I thought about my mother and father. When they were hurting me, I thought about stupid things, like Mr. Rocher's science class, and my upcoming egg drop experiment. We had to drop an egg off the side of our school building and somehow prevent the egg from cracking when it hit the ground. *How would I do it?* I wondered.

"If you want to save the egg from cracking, you must create something to break its fall…it needs protection at all times," I could hear my father's voice instructing dryly. But there was no one to protect me. Not in this hellhole. Not anywhere.

I dreamt about Sunday dinners and church outings. But then most days, I would remember where I was, and that I would never be going back home, to church, or science class again. I thought about the egg cracking, and then I thought about Claire's delicate face. I didn't protect her; she's broken…

There were days when nothing happened, when no men came and no one bothered me. One time, I spent the entire day lying on a fake-leather sofa, following the cracks on the wall with my slanted eyes. It was like a maze I was trying to get out of; if I followed the cracks long enough, they would show me the way out. That day in particular, I think they forgot about me, because I lay on that couch for so long I started wondering how long it would take for my body to stick to the slick surface of the couch. My skin and its plastic fibers were molding together, growing together as one, like symbiosis, or whatever it's called. I tried to force myself to move, staring down at my useless legs and arms. *Get up*, my brain would say, but my body resisted.

When I was up walking, gravity pulled me down, pushing on my shoulders and pulling at my legs, making every step feel painful, heavy, and slow. I couldn't help thinking about that expression, "The weight of my burden was too much to carry." I certainly felt like I was carrying something around, something that felt like a two ton steel ball. I wore that ball around my neck, dragging my feet from one room to the next, unable to accomplish much.

They kept me sedated and zombie-like. I didn't recognize any of the men that came and went, except the one Jeanna called Garrett, the same guy who kidnapped me from the skating rink. He oversaw the other men who came in to see me, but thankfully, never touched me himself.

One night, I awoke in the dark, seemingly alone. "I really did like you," said a boyish voice from somewhere in the room. Before I could answer, the door to the room opened, and I watched the silhouette of a boy leave the room. I wouldn't swear to it, but the voice sounded like Joey's.

***

One night, when my head was the clearest it had ever been in this house, I was brought out of the room and taken to an eat-in kitchen area. Jeanna was seated at the Formica table, waiting for me. The man who escorted me was unfamiliar.

I took a seat across from her. Even though I'd been at this place—The House of Horrors I'd begun calling it—I didn't recognize this room. Everything around me seemed shiny and new since my vision was clear, like when someone with poor eyesight puts on a pair of glasses for the first time.

A plate sat before me, filled with what looked to be meatloaf, mashed potatoes, and some mystery vegetable. The man left the room, leaving Jeanna and I to dine alone. I ate without looking at her, shoving the food in my mouth, barely chewing it. I was ravenous, filled with the kind of hunger I'd imagine waking up with after a long stint of being unfed in a coma.

Jeanna didn't speak until I was done with all of my food. Finally, when she did talk, what she said made me drop my fork with a sharp clang. It hit the corner of my plate, banging loudly onto the floor below. I didn't bother picking it up.

"I'm letting you go now." I will never forget those words. Neither of us moved for several moments, but then she handed me a small purse from next to her chair and pointed to a suitcase that sat near the double oven stove. "There's a thousand dollars in the wallet and a suitcase filled with clothes and toiletries," she said flatly.

"So, what? I can just walk out of here?" I asked incredulously.

"You'll ride blindfolded. One of my men will take you and drop you off. Where you go from there is your business," she said, tapping her long, lacquered nails on the counter impatiently. After everything she'd put me through, now she was letting me go? Nothing about this made any sense. It felt wrong. Like some sort of trick.

"And why the money? I'm not a prostitute," I told her frankly. She shrugged. "You earned the money, and you'll need it to get home. Or to go wherever you'd like," she answered plainly. It was my turn to shrug. "Well, in that case, I'm ready to go now," I said, scooting the chair back noisily and standing up straight. My legs suddenly felt lighter, more airy, and my thoughts were my own, not dreamy or confused.

I walked over to pick up the wallet. I half expected her to get up and stop me, but she remained in her seat, sipping a glass of water quietly. I took the purse and I went over to retrieve my suitcase. "Thanks for nothing," I said, staring at her face, a face I once considered beautiful.

"Before you go, we have a few things to discuss," she said abruptly, stopping me in my tracks.

I knew it was too good to be true, I thought

tiredly.

She said, "Your mother, Barbara, and your father, Thomas, think you ran away. Your father works at a sanitation plant and your mother's a hairdresser. Your favorite cousin, Andrew, goes to Plainview High. I can list off your other family members, where they work or go to school, if that's necessary." She continued to rap those stupid nails on the table, as though she wanted to get this over with. As though giving me a few precious moments of her time was so much to ask. I hated this cold-hearted bitch.

When I didn't respond, she started talking about my cousin, Kara, listing off her class schedule at Nightingale Middle School. I sensed that she was expecting a reaction from me, but I wouldn't give her the satisfaction. "What's your point?"

"My point is that I know everything about you and your life. If you go to the police or tell anyone, I will hunt you down and kill your entire family, and then I will kill you. I'll have people watching you at all times, no matter where you go," she warned, holding up a steady finger, her way of trying to scare me. I rolled my eyes. I was past the point of intimidation. I knew what this woman was capable of; I didn't need any warnings.

"And Claire's parents? What do they believe?" I demanded, clutching the suitcase to my chest. She winced at the sound of Claire's name. "They also think she ran away," she replied softly. Pursing my lips, I stared into her evil eyes, challenging her wordlessly.

"I could kill you, Wendi. But I would prefer not

to. In fact, I've been clearly instructed not to. I do what I'm told, and you should too. Either way, you're not walking out that door until I have your word that you'll keep your mouth shut," she said, a pleading quality to her voice.

I took a deep breath and exhaled noisily. "I won't say a word. I promise," I swore, as much as it killed me to say it.

"One more thing," Jeanna said, standing up and walking over to the kitchen counter. She lifted a small, orange flowery boombox, and she handed it over to me. I looked at her strangely. "The gift you were carrying when you came here. I'm sorry. One of the guys thought it would be funny to unwrap it," she explained. I stared at it sadly, thinking of my mother.

I tucked the wallet in the back of the sweatpants I was wearing, leaving the purse behind. I stood there, holding my suitcase and boombox, waiting for whatever came next.

Jeanna stood there too, like she expected me to hug her or something. Finally, she lifted her hand and I half expected her to smack me. Instead, she placed a finger under my chin, and lifted my head up, making my eyes meet hers. "Keep your mouth shut," she said, speaking slowly and clearly. I understood her perfectly, and I believed her when she said she would go after my family.

Moments later, I was blindfolded and led outside to a vehicle I couldn't see. The person who led me away from the house was a man. I could tell by the roughness of his hands on my forearms, and the stench of his sweat as he moved.

He nudged me into the back of a vehicle. I wondered if this was some sort of sick trick, and they were taking me away to kill me. Shuddering, I imagined my parents finding me in an abandoned field. No, Jeanna wouldn't do that...They were too smart to leave me somewhere dead out in the open, I tried to assure myself. *Maybe they'll just toss you in the river*, a voice in my head said. I shivered again, my teeth chattering uncontrollably. I thought about the gushing waters of the Ohio, my body drifting all the way to the Mississippi. From the Mississippi River, my body would float on down to the Gulf of Mexico, the uneaten parts of my body surfacing in the grassy wetlands for the seabirds to peck at...

We rode in silence. Everything in my visual field was dark, even though I tried to peek out from under the blindfold. I would have tried harder to see, but I was afraid if he caught me peeking he might just shoot me dead. In my head, I counted the minutes until I was dropped off.

Six hundred seconds is what I came up with, which was about ten minutes, right? Suddenly, the vehicle screeched to a halt and I heard the car door open. I waited for several spine-tingling seconds, the pounding of my heartbeat vibrating my ears and chest.

I was yanked out of my seat and I hit the ground knees first. Rocks stabbed at my kneecaps. There was the scuffling of his shoes behind me as he tossed what I knew must be the boombox and suitcase on the ground.

I was left on the side of a dirt road with my

meager belongings, the blindfold still covering my face.

Chapter Ten

I sat there on my knees for a few seconds, afraid to take the blindfold off. I was afraid if I saw my captors, they would just shoot me dead on the spot. When I removed my blindfold, I blinked hard, recognizing the street as the one where "Jed" picked us up that first night in the limo. The skating rink was only a few blocks away from the drop off point. I looked around warily, trying to see which direction my kidnappers went, but the street was deadly silent and void of any cars, except the few stationary vehicles parked in front of houses. Even carrying the heavy boombox and suitcase, it only took about fifteen minutes to walk to the skating rink.

When I got there, I paused in front of it, staring dubiously at the small concrete pad where I'd sat that night, waiting for my mom. How long had it been since that awful night? A few days? Months? I couldn't say for certain. It felt like it'd been ages.

My stomach was in knots, a cold sweat dripping down my backside, saturating the butt area of my sweat pants. It was not the fact that I was standing in front of the scene of the crime causing these symptoms, either. Something else was going on with my body, and I knew what it was precisely. My body needed the heroin they'd been feeding me.

I was agitated, achy, and weak. I felt hot and cold at the same time, unable to regulate my own body temperature. I tried rolling up the sleeves of my shirt, and eventually the legs of my sweats. But then my body would alternate to feeling cold, so I'd pull the sleeves back in place and wait for the sweating to return. I kept sneezing and coughing uncontrollably, choking on what felt like a lump in my throat. I felt deathly ill.

All I knew was that I needed the heroin right then, and I could have used the money Jeanna gave me to look for some, but who in the world would sell a young girl heroin? I realized at that moment I was an addict.

I walked nearly two miles, the bus station emerged from the distance like a welcoming beacon of light. When I got there, I used the money Jeanna put in the wallet to buy a bus ticket to Albuquerque, New Mexico. Why New Mexico? Because I'd had a dream about it once.

Selecting a seat in the back, I shifted around on the plastic seat in agony, wishing the pain would go away. People were probably looking at me like I was crazy, but I honestly didn't care. I was too exhausted to move, but too edgy and irritated to sleep. The hours of that ride ticked down miserably, and I wished the entire trip that I'd chosen a closer destination point.

There was a children's rehab center in New Mexico, but by the time I made it to their front stoop, my entire body was writhing in so much pain and discomfort that I was gritting my teeth, unable to speak.

Eventually, I identified myself to them as a homeless youth, whose parents had died from a drug overdose six months ago. I told them my name was Elsie. I don't know where the name came from. Or maybe I do...a stupid children's book I read in third grade: the story of a poor little fat girl that took everyone's lunch money to buy candy. All of her classmates called her awful names, like "fat" and "gross," but I always liked her character. I felt sorry for her, even pitied her. Maybe I wanted everyone to pity me. The name fit me perfectly. The girl who didn't fit in. The misfit everyone felt sorry for.

The ladies at the rehab center took me in and kept me for sixty days. They relieved my symptoms with a medication called Suboxone. It provided cool, calming relief to my dreadful withdrawal symptoms. I said nothing to no one about my kidnapping.

The first thing I did when I felt well enough was lift two sets of prints from the boombox using tape. I had Jeanna's fingerprints, even if I wasn't ready to go to the police. Someday, I would handle this on my own, I decided, bagging up the printed tape in a Ziploc. I hid it all in my personal cubby space, guarding it like a precious gem.

In the meantime, I couldn't take the risk of going home. Even if I'd wanted to, I no longer had a choice. I'd already told them my make-believe story about my parents' overdose, and my case manager there had contacted the proper authorities.

After my sixty days was up, I was whisked away from the inpatient center by social services, and Elsie McClain became a ward of the state.

Chapter Eleven

I arrived at Saint Mary's Home for Children two days after my fourteenth birthday. I'd come to the realization at the rehab clinic that I'd spent half a year in that house of horrors in Flocksdale. It was hard to believe that so much time had passed, and I'd spent all of it in a drug-induced stupor.

I missed my family. When I thought about my mom and dad, I tried not to imagine the looks of devastation on their faces when they concluded I was a runaway. Maybe someday I'd feel safe enough to go to them, but until then, I was stuck living in a foster home.

Never in a million years had I imagined I would live somewhere like this. There were five boys and four other girls in the home at first. The four of us girls slept together in a cramped twenty by fourteen room. We slept on worn out wooden bunk beds barely an arm-length apart. The floors were dusty, the ceiling covered with outdated, peeling wallpaper.

Even though the space was cramped and sparsely

furnished, I felt safer than I had in a long time. The more people around me, the better I felt. I was afraid of being alone with my thoughts, or venturing out into the world. It's a strange feeling being afraid of yourself and other people. It leaves you in a constant state of limbo.

I avoided talking to anyone the entire first year I lived there. I was afraid to get close to anyone for fear that Jeanna and her cronies were watching me. It seemed crazy and paranoid to think they could reach me here, so far away in Albuquerque, but I believed it nonetheless. Sometimes, especially when I first arrived, I would peek through the cracks of the window blinds, making sure that limo wasn't parked outside, and none of Jeanna's cronies were surveying the foster home. I was scared all of the time, living on the edge of a bottomless pit of fear.

I didn't want to get anyone hurt, like what happened with Claire. If I'm being honest with myself, I also felt afraid to talk to the others because I felt like I couldn't trust them either. Suddenly, everyone around me looked unscrupulous and capable of malicious behavior. I was nervous and on edge, and every little sound made me jump out of my skin. I woke up every night sweating and panting, sometimes screaming. There was a doctor and a therapist that visited often, and they prescribed me a small handful of anxiety pills that the ladies handed out to me morning, noon, and night.

The doctors and foster care staff knew something was seriously wrong with me. I was exhibiting classic signs of post-traumatic stress. However, with the story I'd told them about my parents, they probably thought the drugs and "death" of my parents was to blame for the night terrors and anxiety symptoms. The therapist urged me to talk about it, but I said very little, only giving out information when I had to. Even when I did talk to them, the information I gave was false.

At Saint Mary's, we received three meals a day in a group mess hall. It was the only time we saw the boys, with the exception of scheduled group outings. The boys were always catcalling at the girls when they saw us. Most of the girls relished the attention, but I kept my head down low. I never wanted to touch a boy again. Or talk to one for that matter.

The lady who ran the place was Ally Mason. Everybody called her "Miss Ally." She was old, nearly seventy, but she had a thick head of black hair and a lovely, still youthful, face. She was kind to me. You hear all these horror stories about the foster care system, but despite my internal fears, I was safe at Saint Mary's. It was the outside world I feared most.

Even the boys, with their perverted remarks and roaming eyes, were essentially harmless. I began to feel more at ease with the place, and even started socializing a bit with the other girls. A few of the girls enjoyed reading and we passed around paperbacks like they were candy, enjoying the stories contained in their pages.

Ally and three other instructors taught us math, science, spelling, and other pertinent subjects. As much as I used to complain to my parents about having to go to public school in the past, now I sort of missed it. I missed seeing friends and teachers regularly. I missed the loud clatter of the lunchroom and the monotonous tone of my least favorite history teacher, Mrs. Martin.

I missed going to the movies and chatting on my cell phone. Most of all, I missed my family. Every Friday night, Miss Ally and a few other staff members took all of us on a group outing. Our outings always consisted of a trip to Walmart in a clunky white van that had 'Saint Mary's Children Services' written across the side. People stared out their car windows, pitying us probably. I always kept my head tucked down low to my chest. I'm not sure if I was ashamed of being an orphan or afraid someone would recognize me. Probably both.

Each of us were given five to ten dollars of spending money, and we were allowed to go off on our own in the store as long as we stayed in pairs. The other half to my pair was always a girl named Georgie Mitchell, because she always had weed or pills to share.

When the group was out of sight, Georgie and I would leave the store and hide out in the parking lot, swallowing the pills without water and taking puffs of the pot. The pills she gave me were stronger than my own anxiety meds, and sometimes they revved me up. I still don't know where she got them. We would roam around the parking lot, peering into strangers' cars, laughing at the contents of their vehicles, or sometimes stealing things if the doors were unlocked.

Sometimes we shopped for a little while, buying

small trinkets with our cash, but mostly I gave her my money for the drugs she gave me. When I did go inside, I would walk through the store, sometimes imagining that I would run into my mom and dad; in the fantasy, they would run toward me, scooping me up in their arms and taking me home with them. I'd pull away from Walmart with my parents, waving good bye to all of the sad Saint Mary's orphans.

But sometimes I imagined seeing Jeanna in the store; she'd grab me and drag me out of the store screaming, shoving me back into that Blazer, my bloody hands leaving a trail through the parking lot.

Needless to say, I preferred to stay at the foster home. I felt safer there.

Every Tuesday, people showed up from the outside world. They gawked at us like we were circus monkeys. Sometimes one of the girls was adopted, but very rarely. Kids our age weren't in high demand.

Whenever one of the girls would leave, another girl was right there to replace her. I tried to be friendly, but I didn't try to make friends, if that makes sense. Nobody could replace Claire—that much I knew for sure.

I failed to meet the eyes of any of our visitors; the last thing I wanted to do was encourage one of them to adopt me. I was content living at Saint Mary's until I turned eighteen. Miss Ally treated me fairly, and I'd fallen into a daily routine that provided comfort to me. Day in and day out, a monotonous—but relatively safe—sequence of tasks.

So, you can imagine my distress when a middle-aged couple turned up one spring afternoon and decided to take me in. Miss Ally came and told me the news in the mess hall. I was having chicken soup for lunch, and I nearly choked on a spoonful of noodles when she gave me the news. I stared down at the bowl, wondering if anyone had ever tried to drown themselves in a bowl of soup. Wouldn't that be a crazy way to die? Could you imagine reading that on a death certificate?

Adoption. What a strange, stupid word. I broke it down into syllables, saying it over and over in my mind until the word itself became meaningless and strange. It was a moment most of the other kids dreamed of, and I know I should have been grateful to be taken in, but going to a strange house with people I didn't know was my worst nightmare.

Chapter Twelve

The Raffertons seemed like an all right couple, despite my previous reservations. They owned an adobe-style home in a small, picturesque neighborhood called 'The Cactus Blossom.' The streets were lined with similarly styled houses. There was a lovely bedroom set up for me with pink frilly curtains, a delicate doll house, and a twin-sized bed. They had no other children.

Baylor, my adoptive mother, confided in me on the first night that I stayed there she had always wanted a child. She and Chuck had tried very hard to have one for several years, but to no avail. Two years ago, Baylor learned she was infertile.

"Why didn't you get a baby, then?" I asked bluntly. I didn't want to seem ungrateful, but I wasn't happy to be there, away from the foster home I'd grown accustomed to.

"Babies are always in high demand in the foster care system. I'm on the waiting list, but in the meantime, I couldn't wait. I wanted a child now. I've learned teenagers are much easier to come by," she replied honestly. I hated the way she talked about us, like we were items on the shelf of a department store. But I appreciated her shooting it straight with me.

My initial stay at the Raffertons' was a trial period; if all went well, they would sign the papers and keep me for good. I was conflicted about whether I wanted to stay or go; at least I was at first. I liked them well enough, but like with most people, I was hesitant to trust them and scared to get close. I imagined sinister intentions in everyone, even the Raffertons. The first few months I was there, I kept waiting for them to pull out whips and chains. There had to be a real reason for bringing me there, some sort of evil plot...but as time went on, I realized they simply wanted me there.

In a way, I resented Baylor for wanting me. Her husband Chuck wasn't so bad. Even though he was pushing forty and balding, something about him was attractive. He was a big, burly man with a barrel of a chest and thick arms. I flirted with him often, and went out of my way to be skimpily dressed whenever he was around. I don't know why I did it. Looking back, I honestly think it was Baylor I wanted to hurt. I resented her more than any man. Perhaps it was because she sort of looked like Jeanna. Even though Jeanna wasn't the one raping me, I hated her above all the rest. There was something about Baylor playing that mother role when I knew she could never be my mother that pissed me off beyond belief.

Despite my inappropriate behavior, Chuck was quiet and kind to me. He didn't pay much attention to me in general; he was always working on his computer or watching the evening news. I suspected Baylor was the one who really wanted me, not him. However, he didn't hurt me, so I appreciated that. Better to be ignored than abused, or so I thought. After receiving so much negative attention from men in my life, being ignored felt kind of nice.

Now that I was out of the foster home, I started to have even more frightful dreams at night. I dreamt of dark shadows lying on top of me, suffocating me in my bed. I would wake up panting, unable to catch my breath. I fought faceless phantoms in the dark. I thought about the lyrics of that damn song, the one they played over and over again in the house.

Baylor was always there to comfort me, but I often pushed her away. One night, she even sat down next to me, clutching a shiny hairbrush in her hand. When she leaned in to comb my hair, I smacked her hand away angrily. All I could think about was Jeanna brushing and curling my hair at the house of horrors, but I couldn't tell Baylor that.

"I'm not some toy for you to fix up and play with," I muttered under my breath. One night, I even shouted, "I'm not your daughter!" and pushed her away from me forcefully. I expected them to send me back to Saint Mary's, but they just kept on trying. I had to admire Baylor's patience and tenacity. Every time I even halfway considered liking her, I thought about my own mother, and I hated myself for it. I was so conflicted, angry, and distant one minute, and then needy the next.

At the end of summer, the Raffertons enrolled

me in high school. At the foster home, Miss Ally had homeschooled us, so this was going to be very different for me. I was nervous, but also excited. At least this way I could get out of that house, the place where people pretended to love me.

Chapter Thirteen

I walked through the halls with my head down. My locker was down a narrow, secluded hallway, and I hung out there by myself at lunchtime most days. I read old paperbacks from the library and camped out in the bathroom a lot. I felt antsy most of the time, a sick feeling in my stomach, like something bad was around every corner.

It was on the third day of school that I met Robbie Simms. He was a twelfth grader with brown, spiky hair and a cool blue jean jacket. "Wanna get high?" he whispered, tickling my ear. I was leaning against my locker, reading a Dean Koontz paperback. A shiver ran up my spine. The last "relationship" I'd had, had begun with those very same words. I say "relationship" because what I had with Joey was certainly phony and insincere.

I should have run for the hills—from Joey then and Robbie now. But I didn't. "Okay," I said, following him outside to the school parking lot, where his beat up old truck was parked. I climbed into the passenger seat and sat with my hands in my lap. The smell of marijuana filled the cab. Unlike the first time I smoked it, this time it smelled strangely sweet instead of acrid.

After the pot, he gave me two tiny blue pills that made me feel spacey and relaxed for the remainder of the day. They reminded me of the pills Georgie had at Saint Mary's. I enjoyed the numbness.

***

Three days later, I snuck out of the Raffertons' house at midnight. I met Robbie two streets over, on Emerald Street. "Where are we headed?" I asked, taking a cigarette from him. "The ridge," he answered vaguely. I shrugged, toking on the cigarette, missing my mother's Newports. As much as I didn't want to be, I was truly scared. There's nothing like being alone in the dark with a boy to bring out those old, familiar fears.

"I was under the impression we were just going to get high," I said stiffly, staring out the fogged up windows.

"We are," he answered, chuckling to himself. He lit a joint and passed it over to me. I inhaled deeply on its end, and I didn't hand it back to him until he looked at me, clearly annoyed. I sighed, passing it over.

Nearly ten minutes later, he pulled the truck over to the side of an abandoned road. "Look," he said, pointing out over the cliff side. It was an awesome view, the city lights twinkling like tiny little stars far down below in the distance. I suddenly remembered sitting out on the back porch at my old house with my mom. When I was little I loved astronomy, even though I thought it was called 'astrology' for the longest time. Mom and I would lay back on a pair of flimsy lawn chairs, waiting, always waiting, to see a shooting star. I couldn't recall us ever actually seeing one, but we enjoyed the sounds and sights of the night sky anyway…

I cranked my window down to get some air. The night air was chilly, but I was burning up. "You got any more of those pills?" I asked irritably. Cutting the engine off, he turned to face me. "Can I get a kiss first, at least?" he pleaded. I thought about it. *A kiss would be okay, wouldn't it?* I nodded, swallowing hard.

He jumped at me, his lips clamping down on mine painfully. He kissed and groped me, his hands rough. I felt hot all over. Pissed off beyond belief. When he leaned in again, I brought my knee up quickly, driving it into his groin. He let out a feminine squeal, and jumped back frantically, clutching his hands around his man parts. I don't know why, but deep down inside me, hurting him brought me some sort of satisfaction.

"What was that?" he yelled angrily. Before I could apologize, he reached out and smacked me across the face. I fell back against the passenger door, shocked by the sting of it. I grasped for the door handle, wrenched the heavy truck door open, and fell out onto the dirt road below. Robbie pulled out of there, tires squealing in the distance, kicking up rocky dust. I was left to walk alone. Another dirt road on another dark night.

Chapter Fourteen

I expected to feel scared as I walked alone in the dark, but strangely, I felt an odd sense of fearlessness. Maybe it was the pot or the pills, or maybe I just had nothing else to fear in life. After all, what worse things could happen to me than already had?

I walked for what seemed like an hour. I kept my head down, watching my feet pound the pavement, counting my steps. Abruptly, a flash of red and blue lights were behind me. I didn't need to turn around to know it was the police.

I took off running, veering off the road into a patch of prickly shrubbery. "Stop running!" yelled a man's voice from behind me. But I didn't stop. I picked up the pace, zigzagging through people's yards haphazardly, jumping over yard gnomes and tearing up plants. I could hear the thump of his shoes, coming up behind me. He was gaining on me.

I darted through two narrow trees, and that's when he took me down from behind. I went down hard on one knee, my face eating the dirt.

He had me pinned. I immediately started kicking and fighting, rolling to my back. Holding me down was about the worst thing that anyone could do to me. I cursed at him angrily, fighting against his rock hard forearms.

"Calm down," a deep, breathless voice said in my ear. "I'm not going to hurt you." He pulled me up to my feet, twisted me around, and held my hands behind my back. The cuffs snapped around my wrists. They were uncomfortable, to say the least. After I was cuffed, he sat me down on my bottom and stood over me with his hands on his hips. The tips of his fingers rested on the gun at his hip.

The officer standing before me did not look a day over twenty. I struggled not to let out a laugh. He had sandy blond hair and a thin, similarly colored mustache. He had an athletic build and a golden, shimmery tone to his skin. He was beautiful.

"Why were you running?" he asked, looking down at me gruffly. *A man like him could keep you safe*, I thought out of the blue.

"I was scared of you," I answered honestly.

"What were you afraid I'd catch you doing?"

"I was making out with a boy in his truck. He got too grabby and I bailed out. I ran because it's after curfew and I didn't want to get in trouble." It didn't get much simpler than that.

"Stand up," he ordered, pulling me back up to my feet. Holding a small penlight, he flashed its tiny beam from side to side, inspecting my eyes. I stared straight ahead, holding my breath nervously. "Are you high?" he asked, his face close to mine. His breath smelled like spearmint gum, a pleasant combination with the smell of his aftershave. I don't know why, but I felt the urge to lean forward and kiss him. After kneeing Robbie in the groin for kissing me, this seemed like a strange revelation.

"Yes. I'm high," I admitted. He grabbed me by my cuffs and led me toward his cruiser. "Please, don't do this," I begged. "I'm a foster kid. If my foster parents find out, they'll send me back for sure." Like a child, I tried to shuffle my feet, slowing down the inevitable.

"I know who you are," he said, catching me off guard.

"Huh? How do you know…?"

"You live two houses down from me. I know your parents, Baylor and Chuck, very well. They babysat me when I was little," he explained. I looked at him skeptically.

"How old are you?" I asked hesitantly.

I expected him to say it was none of my damn business, but surprisingly, he said, "Twenty-two."

I couldn't help it. I smiled and chortled softly.

"Listen, I'm going to let you go. But if I catch you running the streets at night or doing drugs, I'll whisk you off to Juvenile Hall without a second thought. Baylor and Chuck are good people for taking you in, and I suggest you treat them with a little more respect," he said sternly. I nodded agreeably.

I walked the two blocks to the Raffertons' house with Officer Milby driving slowly behind me. I couldn't help it; I liked him. The cruiser moved along at a snail's pace, but I took my time walking back. I enjoyed knowing he was back there, protecting me. I'm like that egg, tumbling off the roof, seconds away from splatting on the ground below, I realized. A failed science project…but for some unfathomable reason, Officer Milby made me want to straighten out my act. He made me want to kiss a boy again.

Chapter Fifteen

That night, I couldn't sleep. The Raffertons were still dozing soundlessly when I snuck back in, but my mind was filled with thoughts of Officer Milby and the way I'd reacted to Ronnie's groping session. Would I ever feel safe with a man again? Or would I always feel fearful and unsure about their motives?

Even though I'd been here nearly two months, I still hadn't unpacked. My suitcase was in the closet, along with that dreaded boombox. Opening up the case, I lifted out the clothes Jeanna bought for me. Even though they'd been washed nearly fifty times at the children's home, I still couldn't get the smell of the house of horrors out of them. They were brand new in the suitcase when Jeanna gave them to me, and I knew the smell had to be long gone. In reality, it was the sight of them that triggered the smell in my mind. A rank mixture of cigarette smoke, damp sweat, and some sort of cleaning agent...I wondered if I'd ever forget that smell.

Sometimes I would be walking down the

hallway at school or moving through an aisle at the store with the Raffertons, and I'd catch a whiff of some boy or man's cologne, and instantly, I'd be transported back to that room. I shivered at the thought.

Sometimes, even the tastes of certain foods reminded me of the house of horrors. Like meatloaf, for instance.

Lying in the bottom of the suitcase was the Ziploc bag containing the set of finger prints I'd lifted from the boom box. I considered the possibility of taking the prints to Officer Milby. But by doing so, I would expose my true identity, and what if they didn't find Jeanna or her helpers? Then my parents could be killed or someone could come take me away again...

I wanted to tell somebody. I wanted to tell Officer Milby. I picked up the boombox and set it down on the bed. I had never turned it on; in fact, I'd barely touched the damn thing. My mother had bought it as a gift for Denver Reynolds' fictitious birthday party. I imagined my mom, pushing her cart through the aisles of Walmart slowly, trying to find a really cool present for me to take to the party. My mother wasn't perfect, but worked hard at being a parent, and that's all any kid could ask for. I missed her terribly. Neither she nor my father deserved what I was putting them through. All those foster kids without parents, and mine were just a bus ride away. It seemed so cruel, knowing they were out there, yet I couldn't go to them.

I imagined them at home, sitting in the living room of our split-level ranch, their feet kicked up in the recliners. My dad always watched the news while Mom read the latest cheesy romance novel. I was always trying to get her to read one of my mystery or horror paperbacks, but she'd just wave me away, declaring that if it wasn't happy or sweet she didn't want to read it. "When you have your own kids someday, you won't want to read that scary crap. Being frightened is no longer fun when there are real-life fears that scare you every day," she'd tell me. For the first time, I got it. After what happened to me, I found no amusement in reading thrillers anymore either.

God, I missed them. Were their day-to-day routines the same? Or had my absence impacted everything in their daily lives? I wasn't sure which hurt worse, the thought of them sitting around crying over me, or the thought of them moving on with their lives.

CDs were lined up on metal racks in the Raffertons' living room. I browsed through the titles, looking for something that sounded familiar. Tom Petty and the Heartbreakers—now that was a band I recognized. When I was young, my dad went through a guitar playing phase. Too nervous to play in front of people, he would test-drive his quiet tunes on me. I guess he figured his little girl wouldn't be too critical. No matter how sharp or flat the notes were, I danced and clapped along jovially. My favorite song he played for me was "Mary Jane's Last Dance." Even now, I could still see his slender, tanned fingers picking at the steel strings of his acoustic guitar as he sung the lyrics to the song softly, hesitantly. I squeezed my eyes shut, willing the memories to fade away, but they clung on anyway.

Someday, I hoped to get back to them, but I had to prepare for the worst—which was the possibility of living with the Raffertons for the rest of my life.

Would it really be so bad? I wondered. Baylor did want me, after all. It was nice to know there was someone out there who wanted me for reasons that weren't ill-intentioned.

I ran my fingers along the rows of their CDs. I considered snatching one to take with me to my room. Then I changed my mind and went back to the boombox, peering at it apprehensively. There was a small compartment on the top of the box for inserting CDs. With a push on its lid, it popped open easily. There was already a CD inside.

A band called The Doors. I stared at it, almost afraid to touch it. I'd never heard of them, but I was leery of anything coming from Jeanna's house. I pressed play, and a sick, awful feeling was forming in the pit of my stomach. When the words rang out, I recognized the music immediately. I would know that haunting voice anywhere.

I skipped through the track until I found the particular song I was looking for. A melancholic voice rang out. Words about the end, and how his only friend was "the end." I shuddered. I wanted to turn it off, but I sat there, frozen, listening to the song from start to finish. Unsurprisingly, it was called "The End."

Why was I torturing myself? *Because, deep down, you deserve it*, a voice inside my head rang out. I shook away the thoughts, clamping my hands over my ears, wishing the thoughts away.

I wondered if the CD was left in there by accident or if it was another form of a cruel joke on Jeanna's behalf. I was tempted to take it out and smash it on the floor, busting it into tiny little shards. But I kept on listening. Images of that black-filled room and the terror I'd felt as I lay there helplessly filled my mind. I'd been so sure they were going to kill me. They didn't; they killed my best friend instead, and now I was stuck here, left behind to pick up the pieces and deal with the weight of her loss.

Eventually, I stood up and turned the player off. Shuffling through my bag, I looked for more tape. I lifted the CD from its tray, thrilled to see two distinct fingerprints on the shiny side of the disc. Bingo! I bagged up the entire CD, careful not to smudge the prints or add any more of my own prints to it. Someday, I'd get her...all of them... "I promise I'll get them for you, Claire," I whispered breathlessly.

I anticipated another nightmare as I drifted off to sleep, but I was pleasantly surprised to have sexy dreams about Officer Milby. It had been a while since I'd dreamt of anything good, and especially anything about a member of the opposite sex. I knew nothing could come of the fantasy, but it didn't hurt to think about it. It felt good, feeling something besides grief, anger, or numbness for even a brief moment.

Chapter Sixteen

I breezed through my sophomore and junior year. Well, I shouldn't say breezed. The time passed quickly, but I struggled with concentrating, and my grades wavered frequently because of it. I also had trouble getting along with the other girls. They called me things like 'slut' and 'bitch,' and I returned the favor.

Robbie Simms never spoke to me again, not after what happened at the ridge, and he told everyone that we had sex. I wanted to spit in his face and stomp on his nuts, but I refrained, determined to do right by the Raffertons, just like Officer Milby had instructed me to.

After that night on the ridge, I'd learned that Officer Milby's first name was Jonathan. He did, in fact, live two doors down from the Raffertons. I did everything I could to get his attention, even sunbathing half nude in the backyard. He would wave and gaze at me briefly, but that was the extent of our interactions. I was certain that an upstanding man like Jonathan had to have a wife and kids, or at

85

the very least, a girlfriend. But he lived alone, according to Baylor.

Baylor and Chuck were nice to me. Eventually, they wanted me to call them 'mom' and 'dad,' but I just couldn't do it. My real mom and dad were out there somewhere, and I would never forgive myself, or my kidnappers, for breaking my parents' hearts.

Maybe someday I'd try to think of them as my real parents, but for now, I just wasn't ready. We ate dinner together like a family and watched old movies on the weekends. My life almost seemed normal. Almost.

All in all, despite some of the difficulties at school, I was doing well. I wasn't using drugs, and I was keeping to myself mostly. But then something happened outside of my control. In the middle of a Sunday dinner, Baylor announced, out of the blue, that she was pregnant. She proudly displayed a pregnancy test—ironically called *Clear Blue* just like her announcement—with two light blue lines. Baylor was pregnant, despite her doctor's earlier diagnosis. The Raffertons were going to have a baby. It was hard for me to wrap my brain around. It was a miracle; it was a tragedy.

I stared at the tiny pale lines, willing them to just go away. If Chuck and Baylor had a baby, where did that leave me? Where would I fit in their family now? I felt angry and sad. But most of all, I felt alone and unwanted.

Chapter Seventeen

Nine months later, Baylor and Chuck brought home a beautiful baby girl. She had chubby, dimpled cheeks. They let me name her Claire. Her eyes were dark, almost black at first, but then they turned a lovely sea blue color, and she had gorgeous blonde hair to top it all off, that curled around the edges of her ears. She slept constantly, barely able to keep her eyes open for more than a half hour at a time. She also ate like crazy, taking bottles almost every two hours. Baylor let me help her and I did sometimes, warming up bottles at feeding time and changing her diaper too.

Baylor loved baby Claire so much, in a way I just knew she could never love me. It hurt to see her so happy, but I was pleased for her and her husband. I don't know why, but I started acting out in a variety of ways.

It all started a few months before baby Claire was born. I didn't come home after school most days and my grades dropped significantly. I fell in with the wrong crowd, a group of roughneck boys from the other side of town. I let them use my body, and in return, I used their drugs.

Deep down, I think I was trying to get them to notice me. The boys in town and the Raffertons. But Baylor and Chuck were so caught up in getting the house ready for the baby and attending ultrasound appointments, they barely seemed to notice my change in behavior.

The Raffertons tolerated everything I did, but not when I brought home the drugs. Two months after the baby was born, Baylor found a small pouch of heroin hidden in my bottom panty drawer. As it turns out, the Raffertons were paying attention after all.

I'd found a local connection through one of the older boys at school. After doing heroin again for a month solid, I'd gone back to feeling addicted. I stopped wanting it and started needing it to function again. There was that same old feeling creeping up my back, making my skin crawl when I didn't have it…

Baylor and Chuck confronted me about the drugs, and I told them the truth. That's when they sent me back to rehab.

***

I was in rehab for nearly six months, and in truth, I sort of enjoyed the solitude. Besides attending group therapy, I spent most of my time on my own, reading or writing in my room. During that six month period, I read some of the best books of my life, like *Lord of the Rings, On the Road, Alice's*

Adventures in Wonderland, Lolita, and *The Great Gatsby.* I also started writing short haikus and silly stories. I never wrote anything scary or sad, just meaningless, upbeat tales of love and friendship.

When the psychiatrist thought I was stable enough to go home, he brought me in his office. "We're releasing you, Elsie," he said, looking at me seriously over the top of his glasses.

"Good. I feel ready. How soon will the Raffertons be here to pick me up?" I asked eagerly. Dr. Gibson took his glasses off and rubbed the bridge of his nose nervously.

"You can't go back there, Elsie. The Raffertons can't take the risk of having you there with the new baby. Miss Ally from Saint Mary's will be here to pick you up in under an hour. You better start packing up your stuff." I should have been upset, sad, or angry at least, but I felt completely numb. Of all the times I'd wanted Baylor to throw in the towel and give up on me, this time wasn't one of them.

Chapter Eighteen

The head mistress picked me up as promised and drove me back to Saint Mary's. I didn't say one word to her the whole way there. The familiar stone pillars and the paint-chipped sign greeted me as I arrived. I was going to miss Chuck and Baylor. I was going to miss baby Claire even more. She was still too young to smile, and every day I would tickle her and smile at her brightly, hoping to catch her first one. I wanted to be there the first time she smiled and laughed. I wanted to be the first one to see her walk. Now, I would never get to see that beautiful baby hit any of her major milestones.

But the reality was that a small part of me felt relieved to be back at Saint Mary's. After all, it was the place where my life as Elsie McClain first began. As soon as we went in, Miss Ally sat me down in her office and pursed her lips, looking me up and down speculatively.

"What?" I asked defensively.

"You're almost seventeen now, Elsie. You have one year to get your life straightened out so that you can begin your new life as an adult." I stared at her, considering her words carefully. I'd not even considered the fact that in one year I'd be on my own.

"You need to finish your education, secure some type of employment, and save up enough money to put down a security deposit on an apartment. Unless you would prefer to be homeless or in jail," she challenged, raising her eyebrows at me provokingly.

I shook my head, staring down at my sneakers guiltily. Miss Ally was kind, but stern, and she always had this way of demanding absolute respect.

Everything Miss Ally said was true. I had to prepare for adulthood. I didn't want to live on the streets or wind up in jail. Also, deep down, I knew I had to get my act together because I had to be ready for the moment when Wendi Wise would take her revenge, reentering the world as herself.

Chapter Nineteen

That last year at Saint Mary's, I held it together fairly well. There were a few incidents involving drugs, but for the most part, I stayed on track. I couldn't have done it without Miss Ally's guidance and help.

She helped me complete the requirements for my high school diploma and set me up with a job interview at a local Costco. Surprisingly, they hired me, no questions asked. I had a feeling that Miss Ally either pulled some strings or threatened the manager's life. I suspected the latter.

I worked nearly forty hours a week, and Miss Ally held onto every penny I earned. She took me to cash my check each Friday, and she promptly took the money away from me, storing it in her personal safe. It was probably for the best; having that much cash on hand, I was bound to go out and use. About a month before my eighteenth birthday, she took me to the bank and helped me set up my own bank account. It was legit, with a debit card and a fat book of checks. I felt so grown up and proper.

I actually enjoyed working. The monotonous nature of checking food items across a scanner and bagging them up mindlessly held an appeal for me. Not thinking was exactly what I needed. Not thinking about Jeanna, Claire, the Raffertons, Mom, Dad, or Officer Milby...

For some reason, Miss Ally was significantly attached to me, and it became obvious that last year at Saint Mary's. She paid extra attention to me, and I watched her watching over me with a worried expression when she didn't think I was looking. On my last day there, she told me why. Her own daughter, Hannah, was my same age when she died of a drug overdose. In pictures Miss Ally showed me, she looked a lot like me.

"I went upstairs to her bedroom, to wake her up for school. She was always smacking at that alarm clock of hers, snoozing for an hour until I forced her to get up. But this day, it was just beeping away...and when I pulled the covers back, her lips were blue and her skin was hard. I'll never forget the way her eyes looked. I held her stiff corpse in my arms until the ambulance came. But of course there was nothing left for them to do..." Miss Ally recalled, her voice far away and tinny.

I wrapped my arms around her, holding onto her a little longer than was appropriate. I thought about Claire's dead eyes, and again, I almost considered telling my story. She was someone who could understand trauma and loss, and I wanted to share mine with her. But I didn't. Losing a friend wasn't the same as losing a child, and I couldn't take the risk of telling.

"Thanks for never giving up on me," I told her. It was my last day at Saint Mary's. I was eighteen now. I pulled away from the home, watching Miss Ally's figure get smaller and smaller in the distance. I was driving a beat up Corolla, but I loved it because it was mine. I babied it, washing its dented fenders and scrubbing its already stained floor boards.

My driver's license was just one more thing on the ever-growing list of things that Miss Ally helped me attain. She helped me study for the driver's exam and took me out to practice in the old Saint Mary's van. "If you can parallel park this big old thing, you can parallel park anything on test day," she'd told me. And she was right. I passed the test with flying colors.

She also helped me apply for a new social security card. I'd concocted this whole story about drug addicted parents, and my mother giving birth to me at home, and somehow they believed me. I was legitimately 'Elsie McClain' on paper. Technically, I never had to go back to being Wendi Wise. Perhaps it was for the best that I didn't. I could simply pretend Wendi died that day in the house of horrors. The truth is that a part of her did; the part that believed in humanity, the part that was carefree and happy.

Miss Ally and I spent the last several months of my stay in foster care apartment shopping, and I'd put down a security deposit and paid first month's rent on a six hundred square foot apartment that was attached to an old-fashioned barber shop below. It was only a half mile from the Costco, which was wonderful because if my car broke down, all I had to do was walk to work.

"You can make it here, Elsie," Miss Ally had assured me when we'd stood inside it together, after putting down the deposit. She was proud of me, and for the first time in a long time, I'd felt a sense of pride in myself. I was going to have my first real place, a safe spot of my very own.

"You can even come visit me whenever you want, since I'm right around the corner," Miss Ally added. I suspected that I would visit often, and I knew with full certainty that she would be checking up on me.

I parked the Corolla in front of the barber shop and climbed the shaky stairwell up to my apartment. Miss Ally and I had spent the past week moving my stuff from the children's home over to the apartment, so it was already filled and homey. My stuff didn't consist of much: a shabby love seat and arm chair we'd found at the Salvation Army, and a table and mattress I'd bought with my own money I'd earned from work.

Miss Ally had given me extra dishes and leftover cooking utensils from the foster home, and I'd bought plenty of food and toiletries to fill the refrigerator and cabinets. It was perfect: a brand new life for my brand new identity. I was Elsie McClain, the *recovered* addict who had her own apartment and worked a full-time job. For once, I felt like something other than a piece of shit drug addict.

Chapter Twenty

My apartment was great till nightfall came. It was the first time, ever, that I'd been alone in a house. Turning all of the lights on didn't help much either. I had a TV equipped with rabbit ears, so I tuned in to a local news station and wrapped one of the tattered blankets that Miss Ally had given me from the foster home around my shoulders. I shivered in spite of its warmth.

I tried to concentrate on the news, but then I got antsy. I was pacing the floors when a loud banging sound on my door was nearly enough to send me into cardiac arrest. I clutched the blanket around my shoulders tightly, wondering if I should open it or just pretend that no one was home. With all of the lights shining brightly in my apartment, that seemed like a poor idea.

I got up and went to the door, peering through the peephole warily. I was hoping it was Miss Ally, stopping by to check on me. But it was a thin, dark-skinned man with a buzz cut and big yellow teeth. The chain was securely fastened to the door, so I opened it a crack and peered at him through it.

"Who are you?" I asked bluntly.

"Terrell, your neighbor. I live across the street in those apartments over there," he said, pointing at a rundown, two-story complex behind him. "Just thought I'd say 'hi' and welcome you to the neighborhood," he went on, scratching his head uncomfortably. When I didn't respond, he said, "I saw you and that lady moving stuff over here last week. I thought you looked kind of cool…"

"Hi. I'm Elsie," I replied awkwardly.

He looked me up and down through the crack, assessing me for something. "Do you get high?" he whispered through the door.

Chapter Twenty-One

My nights were plagued with nightmares, and the drugs Terrell gave me didn't help. I dreamt of massive, crawling snakes that turned into the faces of men with long, slithering tongues. Sometimes I dreamt that I couldn't move; I was stuck to the floor, but when I looked at my wrists and ankles, there were no shackles. Just me, holding myself prisoner.

Sometimes Terrell gave me what I wanted, which was opiates. But mostly he had his own drug of choice, methamphetamine. You could smoke it, snort it, shoot it...I did all three. I liked meth because it prevented me from sleeping and therefore, protected me from those hideous dreams. But the bad thing about meth is that after so many days of not sleeping, it's like you're awake, but dreaming. The snakes came while my eyes were open, which terrified me even more.

Miss Ally tried to visit me several times over the

next couple months, but I was too afraid to open the door. I hid in my closet, taking long tokes of the dreadful drug, wishing she'd just go away and forget about me once and for all. Sometimes I think it was *my* goal to forget about me.

I lost my job at Costco. I didn't get fired for not showing up; in fact, I lost my job because I *did* show up, only I was acting plumb crazy. I thought the customers were zombies, and I ran through the aisles knocking over cereal boxes, and then army crawled beneath the boxes and hid. My supervisor—who was also a zombie—pulled me out from the wreckage and called the police. It was Officer Milby who showed up. I simply couldn't believe it.

He loaded me into the back of his patrol car, but instead of taking me to jail, he took me back to rehab. The worst part of that day wasn't the zombies, losing my job, leaving my apartment, or going back to rehab—it was when I leaned in to kiss him, and he promptly pushed me away. I felt humiliated and totally rejected by him. By everyone in fact...

Chapter Twenty-Two

It was not my first—or second—stint in rehab, but it was my first time in an adult institution and it was, by far, my longest stay. It was called Lady of Hope Pavilion, and it was full of addicts like me. This particular institution didn't believe in treatments that involved symptom-reducing drugs, like Suboxone or Methadone, so I rode out my withdrawals on a stiff, mesh cot, writhing in pain and discomfort.

It was hard to believe that a few months of daily use while living at the apartment could put me back in this state. Truthfully, the withdrawals weren't as bad as the first—or even the second time—I'd gone to rehab. I withstood the pain like a champ, reminding myself every day that I deserved every bit of it. *This is what you get for going back to the drugs*, I reminded myself harshly. I felt tougher this time around. Maybe it was because this time, I'd known what I was getting myself into. I never wanted to be here again. I *will* never be here again, I told myself daily, riding out the worst of it.

When I arrived at LOHP, as they called it for short, my once curvy frame had been reduced to ninety-two pounds. I couldn't believe my eyes when I stepped on the scale. At first, I was convinced it was some sort of trick scale, like one of those silly carnival attractions. *Step right up and observe the amazing, shrinking drug addict! Eventually she will wither away into dust!*

Let's just say all those nights spent without food or sleep finally caught up with me. They'd definitely taken their toll on my body. My first week of painful withdrawal symptoms brought me down another ten pounds, but I slowly started to gain it back as I began to feel better. Food and sleep became welcome companions.

When Dr. Dirk, the resident psychiatrist, determined I was well enough to leave the critical unit—otherwise known as the "dry out" beds—he put me in a room with a roommate. Her name was Remy, and I truly adored her. Remy had pale blonde hair and amazing blue eyes, and she talked with a thick Southern accent. As it turns out, she was originally from a town called Jacksonville, which was less than a day's drive from where I grew up in Flocksdale.

Remy was in LOHP because she liked benzodiazepines, particularly a drug called Xanax. According to her, her mother and father had forced her to go rehab.

"But you're over eighteen," I said, confused by her claims.

"Yeah, but they still support me financially. I'm going to college, you see. Training to be a nurse. They threatened to kick me out and stop paying for school if I didn't go to treatment," she admitted.

"Why did you do it? It sounds like things were going well for you at home. I wouldn't think a girl like you would need drugs to cope," I said, curiously.

She explained, "Well, I didn't need the drugs at first. Actually, my life was pretty great for a while…but then, I was raped by a family friend in high school, and my head's been messed up ever since. I felt like I needed the drugs to dull the pain." I was surprised by the ease with which she confided in me, and I felt an instant connection to her because of her background.

Remy talked to me about her rape, describing it in detail, and even discussed it openly in group therapy with the rest of the patients at LOHP. Parts of me admired her—and parts of me hated her for her candidness. She was amazingly strong, and just being around her gave me my own type of strength. At the same time, she reminded me of my own weaknesses.

As it turned out, Remy was the closest thing I'd had to a friend since Claire died. We ate our meals together and stayed up late, whispering about the boys at the clinic we deemed as cute.

Three weeks later, I told Remy the truth about me and my own story. It flowed out easily, and it felt good to finally tell someone. It was after midnight on a Saturday when I told her. We'd been up late, painting each other's toenails and filling out one of those childish Mad Lib games. She was blurting out one dirty adjective after another to fill in the story lines, and out of nowhere, I said, "What happened to you…it happened to me too."

She urged me to tell her everything. I thought that if and when I ever told someone the truth that I'd water down the story and leave out the terrible parts, like what I saw happen to Claire. But I didn't with Remy. I told her all of it, even the grisly, shocking details of Claire's death. Some of the things I told her I'd barely remembered myself until I said them aloud. Remembering my time spent in that house was terrifying, but getting it out of my head and into the open felt like an enormous relief.

"Your name isn't even Elsie?" she asked suspiciously when I was done. She lowered her voice to a whisper.

I shook my head. "It's Wendi," I admitted, smiling. It felt good to say my real name aloud. I'd gotten so used to being Elsie that I was starting to forget my own real identity.

"You have to go to the police. What about your parents? What about your friend who was murdered? What about *her* parents? What if there are other girls trapped there?" she asked, her eyes widening in fear. Her questions were giving me a headache. She asked a few more, but I wasn't listening. In fact, I'd resorted to my old habit of covering my ears with my hands, blocking out real voices as well as imagined ones.

I'd never considered the possibility of other victims. Or maybe I had, but had just pushed the thought aside because I didn't want to believe it.

The way Remy was looking at me now, I could tell she thought I was a bad person for running away from the truth. Hell, maybe she was right. My list of redeemable qualities was getting shorter by the day. But I'd told her my story in confidence because I'd trusted her. In truth, I'd wanted her sympathy. Maybe I even wanted her pity. But I certainly didn't want a guilt trip.

"Even if I went to the police, I have no accurate information to share with them, and I don't have any physical evidence," I whined. That last part was a lie. I still had the fingerprints I'd been saving for years now. "Plus, they threatened to kill me and my parents."

"But that was almost seven years ago. You are almost twenty now, Wendi! It's time to go forward. It's time to call the police," she urged softly, reaching out to take my hand. I yanked my hand back from her and stood up abruptly. "No!" I shouted loudly. "And you better not tell anyone! It's not your story to tell!" I added, angrily.

I was so pissed off at Remy's reaction that I vowed never to speak to her again. Who did she think she was, sitting on her high horse? Did she think her rape story was better than mine? That she was a better person because she turned in the family friend who molested her, and I did nothing about mine?

I thought about those questions for hours on end, sitting on my cot by myself, and later when I was standing in the shower. Somebody was always watching us, making sure we didn't try to off ourselves. I'd gotten so used to it that it didn't bother me anymore. The woman who was watching tonight was one of those young, churchy, stiff-backed types. I stuck my tongue out at her childishly. What did she expect me to do? Gag myself on a bar of soap?

Maybe Remy *was* better than me. Maybe she was even right. I don't know why I was stupid enough to think she wouldn't react the way she did. Her story ended differently than mine, and because of that, she didn't understand where I was at or what I was going through. I considered forgiving her. I considered *never* forgiving myself. I should have told someone the truth, and that is the real, awful truth that I wasn't ready to accept.

I was worried she might tell my story to someone else, one of the staff remembers at the clinic, or a worse possibility…she might call the police. I considered begging her not to tell, but my pride wouldn't let me do it. I avoided her like the plague.

Two days later, my fears were realized. I was sitting on my bunk, staring out the window, trying to make out shapes in the clouds, when I saw a police cruiser pull into the lot. Officer Milby stepped out.

Chapter Twenty-Three

Officer Milby was not alone. Miss Ally was with him, much to my dismay. I was too ashamed to see her. She'd helped me get my life together and believed in me wholeheartedly, and I'd blown it all within the first year. In fact, if I'm being honest here, I'd started blowing it the first day I moved to the apartment. I'd lost my job and my place. I'd even lost my furniture and most of my meager belongings she'd helped me collect. I was a loser and I couldn't face her. Not to mention the fact that I knew Officer Milby was here to discuss the story I'd shared with Remy. I had to get out of here, and quickly.

Luckily, I still had the boombox and a backpack filled with personal items, particularly the bag with the fingerprints. I hated to leave the boombox behind, but as long as I had the prints, did it really matter? It's not like I wanted to listen to The Doors anytime soon anyway. I also didn't mind leaving behind that dreadful suitcase Jeanna had given me either. I slipped the pack on my back, preparing myself for what I had to do next.

I watched through the window as Miss Ally and Officer Milby approached the building. They were talking heatedly amongst themselves, wearing worried expressions. Within minutes, they would be in my room, asking questions about my supposed rape and witness to a murder.

I had no doubt Remy was responsible for this. She had violated my trust, just like everyone else. I know she thought she was doing the right thing by telling, but right now I could just kill her for it.

I stood up, tightening the straps of the backpack. I took off running down the hallway, keeping my eyes fixated on my feet. If I fell down now, I might not make it out in time.

I could run out the exit in the back. LOHP did not have a court order to keep me here, so they technically couldn't force me to stay. But if a policeman wanted to question me about an old murder…well, that was a different thing entirely. I had to get the hell away from this place.

I slammed into the heavy metal exit door and took off running across the rain-soaked blacktop. My feet sounded good on the thick pavement.

I had no idea where I was going. "I can't help you if you won't talk to me, Wendi!" I heard a voice shout out from behind me. I didn't have to look back to know it was Officer Milby. He was pretty far away, but not too far to catch me. *He called me Wendi*, I realized, panic rising up through my chest.

I kept running anyway, putting more distance between me and LOHP. I expected him to chase me down, but he didn't. Part of me hoped that he would. But like usual, I was on my own. Again. *Just as it should be*, I thought breathlessly.

Chapter Twenty-Four

I had no money and nowhere to go. I walked until the sun disappeared beyond the horizon, and then I stuck out my thumb on the side of I-65. It was a cold, drizzly night on the cusp of winter. If I stayed out here too much longer in my thin, knitted tee, I'd be sick with pneumonia for sure.

I didn't expect anyone to pick me up, but surprisingly, a truck driver pulled over around midnight. It was one of those enormous big rigs, and he was pulling two trailers behind him. He waited patiently for me to climb up into his cab.

"Hey, there! I'm Mick. Where ya headed?" he asked cheerily. Mick was nearly ten years older than me, with a beer gut and grayish brown hair. He had a thick country accent that made Remy sound like a New Yorker.

I climbed into the cab, grateful to accept a ride from anyone in this weather. "Anywhere but here." It sounded like a great movie line, and it was the

109

truth.

Mick was a commercial truck driver, and I spent the next five months roaming the countryside with him. It felt great, belonging nowhere. In a one year period, I visited nearly all fifty states. I felt lucky and free, like a wanderer that belonged nowhere, but everywhere at the same time. I was wild and free.

Mick was gentle-natured and had one of those go-with-the-flow hippie attitudes that I sort of loved, and sort of loathed. There were a lot of great things about Mick. But like most of the men in my life, Mick was heavily into drugs. He liked any drug that sped him up and kept him awake on the road. He got paid by the mile, so there was a lot of incentive for staying awake and driving as much as he could.

Heroin was still my thing, and I eventually got him hooked. We charged down the endless highways, revved up on coke, speed, or heroin. Sometimes we did all three. Eventually, being on the road made it hard to establish trustworthy drug connections, and after being ripped off a half dozen times, we started to reduce our traveling schedule.

For a three month stretch, we stayed at one of those rent-by-the-week campgrounds. It was barely March when we first got there, and we nearly froze our asses off in a tent. We could have slept in the truck, but it was uncomfortable and we were determined to camp. It seemed like a fun idea at first, but then it just seemed miserable.

When Mick and I were high, we could stay up all night, hanging out around the campfire, telling stories and philosophizing on life. But when we weren't, we couldn't stand the sight of each other, and we'd roam around the campground aimlessly, waiting for our next score.

The thing about Mick is that he was a veteran of the Gulf War. He never talked about his time spent there or what he did exactly, and he never asked me about my trauma either. I think that's another reason why we liked each other; we'd both been through some shit but we never bothered each other with the details. Eventually we ran out of money, and Mick needed a steady trucking job.

We decided to settle down, and try to stay somewhere permanently that didn't involve using a tent. He got a job driving for only a few days at a time for a local trucking company in Albuquerque, which gave us some time to be stationary. It also gave me some time to myself on those nights when he was away. I spent a lot of time thinking about Claire and my parents again. There's just something about being alone with my thoughts that has always driven me crazy.

I don't know why I went back to the drugs after rehab. Running away from there and right in the arms of another user was just my luck. The drugs and the men...never a good combination for me. The truth is, I think I unconsciously selected men that were users. Maybe it was how they carried themselves or their overall appearance. Or maybe it was the way they spoke. I really don't know. I don't think it was all me though. I think men like that were drawn to me as well. It was like two fast moving train cars crashing into each other at the speed of light…

Our apartment was a dump. Furthermore, my life was in shambles. The last thing I wanted to do was go back to rehab, but I was on the cusp of my twenty-first birthday, and I had a deadline to keep.

I'd hit a turning point in my life. Maybe I was simply just burned out from the drugs and hard living. Maybe I was sick of taking drugs that no longer made me feel high, and only made me feel "normal." I woke up feeling awful, and I needed the fix just to reach a semi-normal physical and mental state. It all felt like a waste. A waste of time and a waste of a life in general.

I don't know what made me change my mind…but maybe it was when I was searching for Remy's telephone number in Jacksonville, and I found her obituary instead. There was no information on cause of death. No need. I knew in my heart she'd overdosed.

***

I still didn't know where my straw was, but I used the dollar bill to take my last hit. It was time to go back to rehab, but this time things were going to be different. For the first time in my life, I had a solid game plan. Step one of the plan was getting clean, obviously, because all good plans require clear thinking. After that, I was going after Jeanna and everyone involved in my kidnapping and Claire's death.

Claire deserved an obituary. Her parents deserved to know the truth. My parents deserved it too. Remy was right all along, and if she was still alive, I'd let her tell me "Told you so."

God knows it was time to go back to rehab. I'd hidden from the world of Wendi Wise long enough, and it was time to go back to the town I'd fled and face down the demons that ran me out.

I'd had enough time to think things over, and I'd come to the conclusion that I wanted revenge more than I wanted any drug, man, or safety net in the world. The other day, I read a catchy quote that said, "I can't drown my demons. They know how to swim." Well, that saying might be true, but if I can't drown mine, then I'm going to slice them up instead. Hence, my sharp set of butcher knives…

Part Two

Chapter Twenty-Five

The End

The doors to the rehab center opened before me and I sucked in deep breaths of cool, fresh air and sunshine. It felt good to finally be free, free of the treatment program, but mostly, free from the drugs.

For the first time in my life I had a plan. Miss Ally had a plan for me three years ago, and it didn't work out on her terms. But this time around, I was the one doing the planning. I'd been through drug treatment before—four times in fact—but this time around I'd taken it seriously. I'd gotten up early every morning and attended every single meeting that was offered at the center. I didn't miss any, not even one. Instead of sitting back and listening to others' stories, I became a leader, speaking out daily about my addiction and traumatic experiences with drugs.

I never told anyone about the rape though, or about what happened to Claire. It's not that I was afraid this time; it was that I wanted to deal with it on my own. Like I said, I had a plan.

My plan would be time-consuming, difficult, and dangerous…but I was ready nevertheless. For the past ninety days I'd been eyeing the McDonald's across the street from the treatment program. My first order of business was to get a job and establish some sort of income.

It was nearly noon when I walked through the door of McDonald's. It was filled with people eating at tables and waiting in lines for their food. It was definitely rush hour for this particular establishment. I had less than twenty dollars to my name, but I ordered a mocha flavored milkshake and one of those dollar burgers.

The place was filled with a greasy aroma, and my stomach rumbled as I carried my tray through the crowd of customers. I took a seat at the only empty table in the back, and I watched the traffic come and go on the street outside, and the foot traffic inside the restaurant.

There were workers dressed in neat, button-down shirts with the restaurant's logo on the breast pocket; they were working the front counter, drive thru, and back line. I knew their starting wage couldn't be much, but it would be enough to get me back on my feet. After all, something was better than nothing.

I also liked the idea of working close to the rehab center. All I had to do was glance out the window at its shiny, red doors and be reminded of what I never wanted to go back to.

When the lines had slimmed down and the tables were cleared, I went to the front counter and requested a job application. The pert, friendly girl at the front dug beneath the counter and produced a crisp, white three-page form. I thanked her and resumed my seat in the back.

I filled it out as honestly as possible, and made up stuff when I had to. Maintaining my fake persona had proven to be more difficult as an adult, but I thought I could manage it just fine. Despite the low pay, the way I figured it, if I could work forty hours per week, I could earn enough money within the month for what I needed.

Primarily, I needed a bus ticket to Flocksdale. Once there, I would need money to put down a deposit on an apartment and the first month's rent, as well as basic living expenses. I would need to get another job in Flocksdale to support myself, and then I would get my revenge. After doing the math, I figured I'd need at least twelve hundred bucks to get started. It seemed like a reachable goal.

Chapter
Twenty-Six

I couldn't start working for a week. They had to run a background check with my driver's license and social security number, which was fine because neither Elsie McClain nor Wendi Wise had ever been arrested, surprisingly. On paper, I was Elsie. Maybe after all this time I would always be Elsie.

I also had to submit to a drug screen, which was also fine because I was, for the first time in a long time, clean. How did I survive for a week with less than twenty bucks and nothing to my name except a flimsy backpack filled with random crap? I stayed at the local homeless shelter. It was a dreary place, but who was I to complain?

I was grateful to have a roof over my head and a couple square meals per day. I had never been to church in my life, but I started praying daily, asking for salvation for all of the terrible things I'd done and was still planning to do.

While I stayed at the homeless shelter, I attended

several AA meetings. They held them every other week day in the cafeteria. People from all over town showed up for them. I'd been to plenty of meetings before, the ones held on the inpatient unit, but these were different: the people who showed up at these did so voluntarily. I listened to their stories and told them about mine. For the first in a long time, I had few, if any, cravings to use. The fact was that my memories of using were more terrible than good, and the trauma I associated with doing the drugs and withdrawing from them was enough to make me never want to do them again.

Whenever I thought about using, I imagined one of those old seesaws you see on primary school playgrounds. On one end were all of the things I liked about using: The numbness. The excitement. The comfort. But on the other end was all of the bad things: Lost jobs. Lost friends. Disappointed faces. Terrible, writhing pain that rattled my bones and scared me shitless.

Needless to say, the bad side of the seesaw far outweighed the good. I never wanted to use again, and this time I really meant it.

***

My first day on the job was sort of a struggle. There were tons of buttons to memorize on the register, and many health-related rules to learn. On my second day, I learned how to make the food, and remembering the different combinations of ingredients was harder than I had ever imagined. Who would have thought that working a fast food job would prove to be so difficult?

I actually did really well on day three, when they put me on the drive thru station. When I didn't have to talk to people face-to-face, I seemed to feel more at ease. I knew how to be polite to people, and I listened to their orders carefully.

"I think we've found your calling, my dear," my manager, Mark Greensburg, announced cheerfully. I smiled at him, feeling a sense of satisfaction.

But my greatest sense of accomplishment came on that Friday when I received my first paycheck. I had received paychecks before when I'd worked at Costco, but this time it was different. This time I got to handle the money on my own, and that paper check in my hand represented so much more.

I had a greater purpose for my money; I needed it so that I could go back to being Wendi, back to being myself.

Chapter Twenty-Seven

I had planned on saving up four checks, but I waited until I had six, just to be certain I had enough money. I saved every dime. My original plan was to just skip town when I had enough money in hand, but I couldn't do that to Mark. Besides my father and a couple others, Mark was the only man in my life who was nice to me for reasons that had nothing to do with sex or drugs. He deserved a proper resignation.

I told Mark the nearest thing to the truth I could manage. I told him I had to return to my hometown of Flocksdale because I missed my family and had personal business to attend to there.

"There are McDonalds' all over the country, you know," he said, when I was finished with my goodbye speech.

I wanted to say "duh," but I remembered he was still my supervisor, and I needed to be respectful.

"What I mean is that I'm sure there's a

McDonald's in Flocksdale. Why don't I put in a transfer request for you?" he offered sweetly.

It was a splendid idea, and would save me the trouble of having to find a new job once I got there. I thanked him profusely, and we got busy filling out the paperwork for my transfer. Everything seemed to be falling in place. It almost seemed too easy, like I was expecting someone or something to screw up. Like myself, for instance.

But I stayed clean and worked hard, and my transfer request was approved on Tuesday night. I hung up my apron, turned in my uniform, and kissed Mark goodbye on the cheek.

The next morning, I boarded a Greyhound bus and headed home to Flocksdale for the first time in nearly eight years. The last time I made this voyage, I'd just been released by my kidnappers. It was a grueling, painful trip that time, but this time would be much simpler. I expected the trip to be meaningful and symbolic for me, but honestly, I mostly slept. I had to get rested for what lie ahead.

Chapter
Twenty-Eight

In some ways, Flocksdale looked just the same as it always had. But new businesses filled in the gaps between old ones, and the roads looked wider, newly painted. The houses were the same. I wasn't ready to go to my parents' house, and even if I was, it was miles away from the bus stop and I didn't have a vehicle yet. Sometimes I missed the old Corolla, but I knew someday I'd have another car to call my own. Lord only knew what happened to it. I never went back to that rundown apartment, afraid Officer Milby would be waiting for me.

Now I had no reason to worry about Officer Milby, but I had every reason to worry about Jeanna and being spotted by local townspeople who remembered me as the missing Wendi Wise.

There was only one McDonald's in the entire town of Flocksdale. It took me nearly a mile to get there from the bus stop, and I was relieved when I saw the familiar arches towering above me in the distance. I went inside and introduced myself to my new supervisor, Andrea Dobson.

Andrea was heavyset but pretty, and she smiled at me pleasantly when I told her who I was. She provided me with a copy of the schedule, which was similar to the one I'd followed before. I'd be working Monday through Friday, alternating shifts, and filling in every other weekend.

I was on the schedule for the next morning. "See you tomorrow," Andrea said, waving me away.

Now was the hard part. I had to find an apartment for less than four hundred a month and it had to be within walking distance from work. I was carrying every bit of cash that I owned in my pocket, and I had this terrible fear of dropping it or having it stolen from me.

There was a small coffee shop and drug store across the street from McDonald's. I looked both ways and took off across the semi-busy road. I went to the drugstore first. I purchased one of those cheap prepaid cell phones that come with minutes already on it, and I bought a single box of hair dye. It had been years since Wendi Wise supposedly ran away, and I highly doubted anyone would recognize me, but I couldn't take any chances. A change in hair color would provide extra protection.

After my purchases, I headed over to a coffee shop. It was one of those hip, trendy locales where kids in tight pants showed up with their laptops, quirky messenger bags, and epic manuscripts. I didn't remember it being here when I was a kid. If only I'd chosen to spend my youth in dull places such as this, maybe I wouldn't have gone through what I did or ran into the likes of monsters like Jeanna, I thought wearily.

I purchased one of their cheaper brews and selected a blueberry muffin that glistened with sugar to munch on. After the lengthy bus ride, I was famished.

I sat down with my muffin and coffee, eating and drinking them slowly. The coffee was piping hot, but I was so dehydrated I couldn't wait, so I sacrificed a few taste buds anyway. When I was nearly finished, I spotted a rack in the corner filled with magazines and newspapers. That was exactly what I'd been hoping for. I spread out a copy of the local paper in front of me on the table, flipping through it until I found a section filled with wanted ads. There were several local listings for prospective renters, and I went to work, searching for my new home.

Chapter Twenty-Nine

The house I found was over six hundred a month, which was way over my budget. However, because of its location, it had to be the one. Additionally, the utility expenses were included, and the ad claimed it was partially furnished. This made the price seem less daunting. It was also further away from work, but again, its location was perfect considering my future plans.

Darkness had fallen, and I headed toward the rental property on Saints Road. I knew exactly where I was going. I also couldn't help thinking how strange it was—the name of the road—after spending so much time in a foster home with the same name. Somehow, I got the sense that destiny was calling.

When I was halfway there, I used the prepaid cell phone to call the number in the paper that was listed as 'Ruth,' who I assumed was the property's landlord. A soft spoken woman answered the call.

"Hello!" I called out, awkwardly. "Ummm…my name is Elsie McClain. I just moved to Flocksdale, and I'm in desperate need of a place to rent. I have the first month's rent and deposit I can give you immediately," I said hurriedly. I had just enough money, leaving only a few dollars more in my wallet.

"That sounds great. Would you like to set up a time to meet tomorrow, or some other day this week?" Ruth asked politely. I hesitated. I didn't want to sound pushy, but I also didn't want to sleep outside tonight. Flocksdale didn't have a homeless shelter; at least they didn't when I was growing up here.

"I know this probably sounds way out of line, but is there any possible way I could pay you and get the keys tonight?" I asked softly. I squeezed my eyes shut, bracing for her response. A car suddenly whizzed by me, and I turned away from it, tucking my ball cap down low to hide my face. I was still paranoid about being seen, and if I had to sleep outside tonight, I was sure to draw attention to myself.

Ruth said, "It wouldn't be a problem, but it's just…I still haven't cleaned up much since the last renters, and I'd need a few days to get it straightened up and move-in ready." I let out a deep sigh. This wasn't going well at all.

"I don't mind a mess, honestly. I'll be more than happy to do the necessary clean-up on your behalf," I offered, grasping at straws. The woman was silent on the line for several seconds. "Okay. If you do that, I'll cut the security deposit in half," she replied graciously.

I tried not to jump with delight.

"Can you meet me there in thirty minutes?" Ruth asked. I smiled broadly. I was already standing in front of the house.

"Sure. I'll see you soon," I squealed happily.

Chapter Thirty

The house on Saints Road was a small, one and a half story dwelling located at the end of a cul-de-sac. The inside was dated, with cheesy brown carpet and wood paneled walls, but I loved it instantly. The bottom floor consisted of a kitchen and living room, and that was it. The second floor had a large, open bedroom and tiny bathroom with a standup shower. There was an old-timey linen closet in the bathroom, built-in shelves, drawers throughout, and a neat walk-in pantry in the kitchen. It also had one of those cool, old-fashioned metal radiators next to the bathroom. I loved its small size; somehow it felt safer than living in a big, grand house, like its walls were hugging me, pulling me close.

Although Ruth had warned me that it wasn't move-in ready, besides a good polish and vacuum, it was clean. I couldn't wait to buy some cleaning supplies and a vacuum cleaner just to do a little sprucing up. For a moment, I actually felt like it was mine. But then I remembered my plans, and I tried to refrain from smiling so much.

For now, all I had was my backpack, which consisted of four outfits—two of which were work uniforms—a toothbrush, a small amount of makeup, a hairbrush, one pair of socks and underwear, my cell phone, my hat, and the finger print baggie with the tape and CD in it. Oh, and the case of knives, of course.

I'd left the knives at home when I went to rehab, and been lucky enough to find the apartment in Albuquerque empty before taking off for the bus. The knives had been in the bottom of my sock drawer, just as I'd left them. Mick was nowhere to be found and I hadn't heard from him since going to rehab. I didn't mind. In fact, I'd barely even thought about him since I skipped town.

Mick and I had had a love/hate relationship; we loved each other when we were high and we hated each other when we were coming down. Simple as that. If truth be told, I'd never felt any sort of real connection with any man. Just as fast as I'd hooked up with Mick, I was just as quick to leave him. I suspected that he too, wouldn't mourn long over our separation.

All in all, I was happy with the new place. Luckily, there were appliances and some furniture in the house. There was a beat up, beige-colored couch and a tiny TV set and a flimsy two-seater table with metal fold-up chairs. Upstairs, there was a full size bed with a lime green comforter and a small night table beside it.

It all seemed fine to me, and I felt an overwhelming sense of gratitude for my landlord, Ruth, as she handed me the keys. "Oh, one more thing to show you," she said abruptly. She walked over to a skinny door in the living room which I'd assumed was another linen closet. The open space revealed a narrow, wooden staircase that led down to a cold, concrete cellar.

"There isn't much down here and it leaks sometimes, but there's a washer and dryer for you down there," she said, smiling at me fondly. She knew I was homeless, that much I could tell. She talked to me like she felt sorry for me, which I was okay with right now. I needed to stay on her good side, and if that meant letting her pity me a little bit, then so be it.

I paid her the first month's rent and partial security deposit. The fact that she had given me a great deal with the deposit, was a relief. Now, at least, I could buy some food and needed essentials before I got my first paycheck. The thought of buying groceries and eating them in my new place was exhilarating. My belly rumbled just thinking about it.

After Ruth left, the house seemed quiet and was filled with shadows. I thought about my first apartment, and how it felt to be alone. Here I was, doing it all over again—only this time I couldn't afford to screw it up again. This time I also had a reason to be fearful. I was back in Flocksdale. Not only that, but I was close to the house of horrors where I was held captive so many years ago. I didn't know its exact location, but I knew it wasn't far.

The windows of the house were small, and combined with the dark paneling, it gave the home a cavernous, secluded feel. I peered down into the cellar below. I shuddered, closing the door tightly. It looked creepy down there, like a dungeon. It was nice having a washer and dryer, but besides when I needed to do laundry, I didn't plan on going down there often.

I walked through the house with its sparse furnishings, wringing my hands nervously. I looked inside the refrigerator; besides a plastic container of baking soda, it was empty. Tomorrow would be a new day, and I would have to get some food after work. There was nothing to do now but sleep.

I double checked that the front door was locked. I turned the lights out and stretched out on the living room sofa. I closed my eyes, making a mental list of all the food I would buy tomorrow.

I tried to sleep, but I felt wide awake. It wasn't fear that kept me going; after everything I'd been through, there wasn't much else to fear—at least that was the conclusion I'd reached over the last few years. I was older now, and braver…I was also free from the drugs, and I had a clear mindset. *You're safe here*, I told myself over and over again. I repeated that word: *Safe*. Had I ever truly felt safe? Yes, I realized. Before that time at the house of horrors, before I'd known how bad people could be, I'd felt safe and comfortable, living my normal, carefree, teenage life.

I got up from the couch and started pacing again, unsure what to do with all of this nervous energy. I could dye my hair tonight, I considered. I thought about it, and then finally decided to do it in the morning before work. I stood up from the couch and crept over to the window. It was dark inside and out, but a lonely street lamp provided a sliver of light that cast a hazy, eerie glow on the blacktopped road in front of the house.

Looking down the street, I was able to pinpoint the exact location of where I was picked up that dreadful day in the limo. This was the street. That skinny, gravel road where I was blindfolded was only a few minutes' walk away from here too.

I thought about that initial ride in the limo, and how I wasn't fearful at that point. I might have been uneasy, but I certainly couldn't have anticipated the horror that awaited me in that horrible house with Jeanna and her minions.

If I'd only known what was about to happen to me…I knew the house of horrors was close. I could sense it. I wanted to start searching for it tonight, but I decided I'd had a long enough day, and I needed a good night's rest. I would just have to force myself to hold my eyes closed until I eventually slept. Tomorrow, my real work would begin.

Chapter
Thirty-One

I woke up at five in the morning, feeling energetic and of a clear mind. I set to work, applying the blonde hair dye. I'd never dyed my hair before, but how difficult could it really be?

I sat on the edge of the sink, with one of four tattered, holey towels that I'd luckily found in the linen closet, lathering my hair with the smelly substance, using thin, plastic gloves. My feet were resting in the sink and my knees were curled up awkwardly toward my middle. The smell of the hair dye was overpowering and it was hard to see parts of my own head, but I finally got it all covered.

I had to let it sit on my hair for twenty minutes, so I sat outside on the concrete-padded porch, watching the sun rise up hazily over the trees. I would kill for a cup of coffee right now. *Or something stronger*, I thought miserably. I instantly regretted that thought, and reminded myself of the seesaw.

I could see the next street over from where I was sitting; so many of the houses looked the same. Substandard houses lined the streets; some were cared for better than others, but mostly they looked alike.

I racked my brain, trying to think about everything I knew about the outside structure and general layout of the house I had been held captive in. I was unconscious in the Blazer when they took me to it, and I was blindfolded when they dropped me off. I didn't know much, I realized sullenly.

I also thought about the house with the steep stairs on the front porch, the one they originally claimed was Jeanna's house, but then she later boasted that it wasn't. It was only a street or two away from here as well. I could remember going there pretty clearly; it was the first place the man named Jed took me and Claire. It was the last time I saw Joey and Zeke, and it was the first time I laid eyes on Jeanna.

It suddenly occurred to me that whoever drove me to the drop off point blindfolded that day easily could have driven in circles to throw me off on the distance we traveled. I'd been terrified and blindfolded, and there was no way to know with any real certainty which direction I'd come from. *There may be no way to trace back my steps to that dreadful place*, I realized unhappily.

Those thoughts made me gloomy, and I tried to push them away. I would have plenty of time to figure out my game plan tonight. But for now, I had to get this damn hair dye off my head and get dressed for work.

***

My hair looked more pumpkin orange than blonde as I took off on foot for work. I was still a little anxious about someone I knew from my previous life recognizing me, so I had my cap tucked down low over my still wet, carrot top head.

It took me nearly thirty minutes to get to work. I slid my time card through the reader, and checked in with my new boss. I was scheduled to work the back line today, for which I was grateful. Hiding in the back was my favorite thing to do at work, and it would especially be my position of choice now that I was back in Flocksdale.

I got busy setting up my station for the breakfast rush, but my mind was on the streets of Flocksdale, particularly the streets surrounding my new rental house. Could I find the house of horrors? If I could, did I even want to? *Yes*, I decided, *without a doubt*. Because it was not the house that I really wanted to find, it was the evil people inside. What would I do if and when I found them? Sure, I'd entertained the idea of using the knives to hurt them. But I wasn't really sure I had it in me to go through with it.

Chapter Thirty-Two

I was on the verge of starving by the time my shift was over. I walked to an old fashioned local food mart only a couple of blocks from my house. On my way there, I passed by the skating rink. It was the first time I'd really laid eyes on it since returning home to Flocksdale.

I expected it to either look the same or be demolished, but it looked like a brand new establishment. A fresh coat of paint and a new name had done wonders for the place. 'Mac's Super Skateland' read the sign in bulky, bold letters on the front of the building. There were smiling children standing with their parents out front, waiting to get through the doors. I looked at them yearningly, craving their happiness and innocence.

Sometimes I wondered how my life would have turned out if I'd never stepped foot in that place. Maybe they would have found a way to get to me anyway, or maybe another traumatic event would have turned up to take its place. *There's just no way of knowing*, I realized. The truth is, bad things happen to everyone at different points in their lives. My life contained some pretty bad ones, but at the same time, I had to pull myself up and live a real life like everyone else at some point. My growling tummy interrupted my thoughts.

I headed over to the food mart, focusing on the grumbling sounds in my tummy. The temperature in the store was icy and crisp, and it felt good compared to the outside heat. There was no point in grabbing a cart. I could only get what I could carry home, which would probably amount to just a few bags. Plus, I couldn't afford much, anyway. Not until I collected more paychecks.

Fresh vegetables and meats looked delicious, but I didn't have pots or pans yet, so I opted to stick to frozen foods I could warm up in the microwave. I strolled up and down the aisles, grabbing what few things I could afford. I selected several Banquet meals, a two-liter of soda, a box of cereal, and a small package of cheap wafer cookies. I couldn't wait to get home and eat every last bit of the food.

The aisles weren't crowded, but there were a few people lined up at the two checkout counters up front. I juggled my items in both hands and under my armpits, struggling not to drop anything as I made my way to the line. I was surprised to see my landlord, Ruth, standing at the end of one line, shoulder to shoulder with a muscular, silver-haired gentleman. He was her husband, I presumed.

For a moment, I stood there awkwardly, unsure if I should approach her or simply pretend not to see her. She saved me the trouble. As soon as she saw me, she stepped out of line, leaving her husband with the groceries at the checkout counter.

"How's everything going at the house, Elsie?" she asked cheerily as she approached. She helped me load my armful of items onto the conveyer belt.

"Everything is going great," I gushed. "I truly love the house, Ruth. Thanks again for letting me move in so spur of the moment like that. I really do appreciate it."

"It's my pleasure. I'm happy to have a new renter," she said, smiling.

She stared down at my food items, noticing them for the first time as the cashier slid them across the scanner. "Will you have dinner with us tonight?" she asked. Of all the things I was expecting her to say, a dinner invitation wasn't one of them. I think I groaned internally.

"No, I wouldn't want to impose," I answered quickly, thinking about my plans to scour the neighborhood this evening.

"Yes, please come. I insist," she said, patting me on the shoulder.

"I don't have a car yet," I added, still trying to get out of this obligation.

"Well, that's okay, honey. We live just a couple blocks over, on Merribeth Avenue. House number 403. Won't you please come?" Ruth pleaded.

"Okay," I gave in, nodding tiredly. "What time?" I asked, handing a twenty dollar bill to the bored looking cashier behind the checkout counter.

"How about seven?"

"Seven it is," I said, grinning at my landlord

through clenched teeth.

I gathered up my few meager bags and made my way out of the food mart, irritated by my freshly made dinner plans. This meant I was going to have to get started late on my little adventure. *Or perhaps*, I considered, forming a new thought...*perhaps, this was a perfect excuse to be out walking around the neighborhood*, I realized cheerily. I could use this dinner with Ruth as an excuse to walk around the streets surrounding my rental house, all the while checking out its occupants.

Chapter
Thirty-Three

Ruth's bungalow was rather small, but well-kept, and surrounded by skeletal trees despite the warm season. There was a narrow, pebbled pathway that led up to a porch covered in sun-bleached wooden planks, where Ruth and her husband were sitting in paint-chipped, Adirondack rocking chairs.

I waved to them, wishing I'd brought something, like wine or flowers, to make me seem polite. One thing my mother taught me was how to be polite. She was always whispering, "Mind your manners," anytime we went out in public or had guests over for dinner.

For this dinner, I didn't have many clothes to choose from, so I'd slipped on a clean pair of work pants and topped it off with a clean, white blouse. However, now I wish I'd just worn jeans, because I could still smell the unmistakable traces of grease on my pants. As I'd quickly learned since starting my job at McDonald's, no amount of laundry soap or softener could erase its fatty, oily smell from my clothes.

"Welcome, honey!" Ruth greeted me kindly. "This is Charlie, my husband." She gestured toward the man in the chair. It was the same man from the grocery store. He smiled and nodded at me cordially. "Come on in." She opened a creaky screen door.

The front door opened into a large, homey kitchen. There was a neat, sleek island in its middle that didn't seem to fit with the rest of the country-styled room. "It smells good in here," I said softly. I wasn't sure what to do with my hands, so I tucked them into my pockets slowly and leaned against the counter awkwardly. Charlie stayed behind on the porch, so it was just me and Ruth.

"You eat meat, right?" Ruth asked, stirring something in a tall white crockpot.

"You're kidding, right?" I winked at her. "Of course. I love meat," I added, warming up to Ruth.

"We're having barbecue, potato salad, and baked beans," she informed me. It sounded terrific compared to my frozen meals at home. My mouth was watering as I peered down at the thin, sweet-smelling strips of meat in the pot.

Ruth had to be around my mother's age, but she looked different than my mom. My mother had always been thin with dark features, whereas Ruth was curvy and fair skinned. She looked like a woman who loved to cook, and she came across as motherly. *I could see her being one of those overly involved landlords if I didn't get off on the right foot with her*, I realized nervously.

"I didn't get to tell you much about me the other night…but, I want you to know that I do have a full time job at McDonald's. It might take me a few months to save up enough money for a car, but I won't have any problems paying my rent, so don't worry," I told her.

"I'm sure you'll do fine, honey," she said, offering me a sympathetic smile. "I'm not worried about you at all, dear. You seem like an honest gal." She gave me a small wink. "Do you have family around here?" I was prepared for questions about my job and financial circumstances, but I wasn't prepared for personal questions.

"Ummm…no," I said. I figured my best bet was to stick with my original lie, the one I'd created in Albuquerque. "My family is from New Mexico. My parents died when I was young, and I grew up in foster care. We traveled a lot, my parents and me, when they were alive that is…and Flocksdale is a place I remember from childhood. For some reason, I wanted to come here when I was of age and could leave the foster care system; I guess I'm just drawn to this town." I spit the story out in a flurry of nervous, rambling sentences.

Ruth was stirring the barbecue in its pot, but she stopped promptly, setting down the ladle beside it. She looked at me sorrowfully. After repeating the lie so many times, I'd gotten used to the pitiful looks.

"What happened to your mother and father? I don't mean to pry…"

"It was a drug overdose," I admitted. I'd gotten so used to telling this story that it flowed out with ease. One time at the rehab clinic, I even went so far as to describe my "dead" parents' tombstones after a peculiar, inappropriate patient asked me to in group.

I hadn't planned on being so forthcoming with Ruth however, when it came to the details of my lie. After all, this was my landlord, not my therapist at the unit. I'd never seriously considered telling anyone the truth, except Remy, of course. *Look how well that turned out*, I reminded myself. Not only did I not want to share my real background with Ruth, but I didn't want to share my make believe back story either. After all, we're not really going to be friends.

"I know all about living with drug addicts," Ruth said, surprising me. "You mean…Charlie?" I asked disbelievingly. The man hadn't said a single word to me yet, but he didn't strike me as an active user. I know them when I see them, and Charlie wasn't an addict.

"No, not Charlie. Don't get me wrong, Charlie and I aren't perfect. We used to drink and dabble in some recreational drugs when we were young, but not anymore. That was a long time ago. I'm talking about my sons," she said softly, turning back to stir the saucy meat.

"Did your sons overdose, too?" I stepped toward the sad woman. She shook her head, swallowing so hard I could hear the lump in her throat.

"My oldest son died in a freak accident. He fell off somebody's roof. But he was high as a kite when it happened, so of course, I still blame the drugs. I always had trouble with him, more so than with my youngest. They had different dads, you see…"

"I'm so sorry for your loss," I said quietly. My parents weren't really dead, but I certainly understood the impact of addiction and what it felt like to lose a family member. My parents may not have really passed away, but they were dead to me, in a sense. I'd lost them so long ago…

I thought about Claire, pushing aside thoughts of her bloody face and limp body on the floor as I looked down through those grates. I thought about Remy, who I felt pretty sure had died of an overdose too. I even thought about Miss Ally's poor teenage daughter, Hannah. So much death…I felt sorry for my landlord, Ruth. She seemed so nice, and to think of her losing her child made my heart ache.

Ruth went on, "My youngest son also has some problems, but he has a job at a plumbing company now and he's staying in one of my rental houses. He's doing well, which makes me happy," she said, perking up.

I helped her set the table, and she filled our plates with the steaming hot food. Charlie came in from the porch and took a seat at the head of the table. He seemed pleasant, but quiet. I tried to force myself to eat slowly, but it was hard to do when the food was so tasty. It was the best thing I'd eaten in years, and it reminded me of my mother's home cooking. My foster mom, Baylor, and the cafeteria ladies at Saint Mary's, had been pretty decent cooks too, but there was no comparison to this. The barbecue melted in my mouth.

"It's so good," I said, smiling up at the couple. When I cleaned my plate, Ruth filled it with another round of barbecue and potato salad. I didn't protest. I ate all of it. Afterward, Ruth filled small Tupperware containers with the leftovers and bagged them up for me. This woman truly was a saint. *The saint from Saints Road*, I thought goofily, drunk from all of the delicious food. I was suddenly glad I'd come over to Ruth's for dinner.

I helped Ruth with the dishes, standing beside her as I dried them off with a polka dotted dish towel. Again, I thought about my own mother, and how doing any activity with her, even something as frivolous as dish washing, would have seemed like a dream come true…

My mother always hated doing dishes. Whenever she heard someone talking about dishwashers and bragging about their latest model, she would retort, "Well, there's a dishwasher in my house too. *Me!*" Then she'd laugh like a hyena, as though it were the funniest joke in the world. *If I ever get to go back home, I'm going to wash all of my mom's dishes for the rest of my life*, I decided suddenly. God knows I owed it to her, considering all I'd put her through.

As Ruth and I were finishing up the last of the plates, she asked, "Do you have any photographs of your mother and father?" I shook my head, being honest for once.

"I left them all behind when I went to the foster home. I wish I did have some. Do you have any pictures of your sons?" I asked, knowing that this woman, of course, had plenty of photos of her family. She seemed like the type of mom that would snap photos any chance she got.

Ruth nodded and dried her hands, eager to show me the pictures. She led me into a cozy, sunken living room, where there was a beautiful hutch filled with silver and gold-framed photographs. I stepped in for a closer view.

"There the boys are together, when they were young," she said, pointing to a photo of two dirty-faced boys perched on their bicycles, grinning mischievously. On the shelf above it was a photo of them as teenagers, and that was the one I couldn't remove my eyes from. Two boys, one blond and one dark-haired, perched side by side beneath a paper birch tree. They wore half-smiles with their arms hung limply at their sides, obviously not too thrilled to have their picture taken. My guess is that their mother coerced them into having it taken. My eyes were glued to the picture of the boys.

"What are their names?" I asked tightly, staring intensely at the photos before me.

"James and Zachary. James is the oldest, the one who died…"

Ruth kept on talking, but I couldn't hear her anymore. The room was spinning. The boys in the photograph were the boys who had identified themselves as Joey and Zeke at the plaza nearly eight years ago.

I took a deep breath, forcing myself to stay calm. I couldn't take the chance of blowing my cover just yet. "This is the one who died?" I asked, tapping my finger on a portrait of the boy who called himself Joey, the one who had given me my first kiss.

"That's him. That's my James," Ruth said breathlessly, as though she hadn't looked at the pictures herself in a while. This one was a school picture, probably taken when he was ten. *Maybe he wasn't evil quite yet at this age*, I considered. *No, I think him and all of the monsters at the house of horrors were born evil*, I concluded.

I didn't care about this woman's feelings anymore. All I cared about was getting answers. "Your youngest son, Zachary…where does he live again?" I asked, swallowing the lump in my throat.

"About a mile from here, on Weston Street, in one of my rental houses," she answered plainly.

"You said the boys had two different fathers. Which one of them was your husband Charlie's son?" I asked.

"Neither," she said, shaking her head. "I got with Charlie after their fathers were out of the picture."

"Does Zachary live alone?" I asked, keeping my eyes on the photo.

If Ruth thought my line of questioning was odd, she didn't let on. "Yes. He lives all by himself, unfortunately. God knows he could use a good girl in his life. But lucky for him, he has lots of family nearby. I own most of the houses on that street, and he has an aunt and several cousins that live close by."

"I have to go," I said abruptly, heading for the door. "Thanks for the meal," I called back over my shoulder to Ruth.

"Do you want me to drive you home?" asked a man's voice from behind me. I froze, standing in front of the door with my back to him. It was the first time I'd heard Charlie speak, and I was certain that I'd heard his voice before. Was it possible that I heard him in the darkness of the house of horrors? I suddenly felt a wave of horror flowing through my entire body, and all I wanted to do was run far away from these people.

Chapter Thirty-Four

Ruth wouldn't take no for an answer. She was adamant that a girl my age should not be walking the streets of Flocksdale in the dark alone, even if my house was only two streets away. If she thought twenty-one was too young to be in this neighborhood alone, I wondered what she would think about my thirteen year old self out there, with her darling sons.

I wanted to gouge their eyes out. But there was nothing I could do but accept the hefty bag of leftovers and climb in the Oldsmobile, taking a seat next to Charlie. We were only minutes away from my house, but he'd become surprisingly chatty. He looked at me differently now that we were alone— he had the eyes of a predator.

I didn't get the sense that he recognized me, but I certainly recognized him now that I'd heard his voice. I was an adult now and I looked completely different, but it wasn't only that. If this man "knew" me, then he knew me intimately, and I tried to imagine his voice in that dark room. Was he one of those men? Is that why the sound of his voice brought chills down my spine and hit me with an undeniable sense of unease? I was certain he had been.

I wasn't exactly sure what role this man played in my kidnapping at the house of horrors, but I knew one thing for certain: at some point during my captivity, this man had been there in that horrible place. His voice brought back images and sensations I'd long since forgotten. I tried to shake them away, taking in slow, timed breaths.

I stared out the window, answering his vague questions about my life with one or two word responses. I couldn't wait to get away from this man and into the safety of my home.

I'd planned on scoping out the neighborhood tonight, but now I needed some time to regroup. My courage was shaken and my head was spinning with the new bits of information I'd received.

"Thanks for the ride home and for dinner," I said stiffly as he pulled into my driveway. I forced myself to smile at him before I got out.

He smiled back at me creepily. "Are you sure you don't want me to walk you in?" he asked.

"I'm positive," I said, closing the car door and shutting him up.

Was I imagining a sinister look in his eye or was it all in my head? I forced myself to walk—not run—up to the door of the rental house. As soon as I was in, I locked it tightly behind me. I slid to the floor, gasping for air. He couldn't possibly recognize me, could he? After all, he'd been in the dark too…surely he didn't recognize my face…

Was I ready for this? Could I face the people who hurt me? Did I have the guts? After tonight, I wasn't so sure.

Chapter Thirty-Five

After my breathing and heart rate slowed, I used my arm to swipe the empty grocery bags and lease papers off my dining table. I walked in the kitchen. Searched for a pen or pencil in one of its drawers. Most of them were empty, but the drawer beneath where the microwave sat held half a dozen writing instruments and a thick pad of lined paper.

I carried my writing utensils to the table. Sat down, then got back got up, closing all of the blinds and curtains securely. I peeked through the slats of the blinds, making sure Charlie was long gone. I started making a small map of the streets surrounding the skating rink. It was time to review the facts.

My street, Saints Road, was two streets behind the skating rink. Nearly seven years ago, I was walking on this same road, supposedly going to Joey's—real name James—mom and stepdad's house, who also would have been Zeke's—real name Zach—mom and stepdad since they were apparently brothers. James'/Zach's stepdad—'Jed'—picked us up in a limo. I made a line with my street's name on it, putting a star by my house, and then another star in the middle of the road with 'Jed' written next to it, noting the spot where he'd picked us up in the limousine.

After that, we rode in the limo to the end of the street, crossed a main road, and drove three blocks over to an adjoining neighborhood. We stopped at "Jeanna's house," but I wasn't sure of the street name and it supposedly wasn't even her house. I drew small lines, making notes of my meeting with Jeanna, and drew a star where I thought the house was located.

We left Jeanna's and returned to the skating rink, which is where I was kidnapped. I pondered, chewing on the pencil's eraser. From there, I was knocked unconscious and woke up in an unknown location. The location of my house of horrors was a big question mark. The most important question mark. I drew a huge mark in the blank space above the roads. I gnawed away at the pencil, mulling over the possible routes again in my mind.

I thought about the ride out of there with the blindfold on, and how I'd counted approximately ten minutes. The dirt road I was dropped off on was between my street and Ruth and Charlie's house on Merribeth Avenue. I marked their house with an X on Merribeth, and wrote their names next to it on my map. I also wrote down Weston Street, which is where Zach—formerly known as Zeke—supposedly lived, according to Ruth. I also made small notations next to Zach and Ruth's names, noting that they were mother and son.

I thought about my conversation with Ruth. What was the name of that street she said Zach lived on? Weston…

Ruth said that Zach lived on Weston Street now, I pondered. I wasn't sure where Weston was, so I didn't write anything on my actual makeshift map. James—formerly known as Joey—was dead. I tried to muster up some sort of sympathy for the guy, as I imagined him lying on the ground with a bent up neck after falling to his death from a roof top. *Serves him right*, I thought bitterly. "Some people just get what they deserve," I remarked aloud to myself.

I tapped the pencil on the table top furiously, staring down at the pathetic map. I didn't know the names of most of the streets, and even the ones I did, I wasn't sure how much of this knowledge was useful to my search. I didn't quite know how to connect the dots just yet.

I pushed the map aside and got a new piece of paper. I started writing down everyone's name that was or could have been involved: James who was now deceased, Zach who lived on Weston Street— Ruth was his mother but his father was unknown. And then there was Jed. What did I really know about him, besides the fact he drove the limo? His address was unknown, as well as his relationship with the other suspects. Then Jeanna—unknown location, unknown relation to others. Jeanna's boyfriend Garrett—also unknown info—the heavyset woman who attacked Claire was also a big question mark.

The random men with their random faces—a big unknown. Charlie, Ruth's husband on Merribeth Avenue. And last but not least, there was Ruth— James and Zach's mother. Her role in my kidnapping/assault wasn't clear. I tapped at the names with my pencil pensively. Stared at my list of names and info.

There was one thing all of the people on the list seemed to have in common besides me. All of them either were, or claimed to be, related. James and Zach were half-brothers. Ruth was their mother and Charlie was their stepfather. Jed was also supposedly a stepfather, and they called Jeanna their aunt.

Perhaps Charlie wasn't their stepfather thirteen years ago, I considered, trying to sort through the details in my mind. Ruth said that both boys had different fathers. Maybe Jed was one of their fathers. But then where did Jeanna fit in? Was she truly one, or both, of the boys' aunt? Or had that just been another bizarre lie in a long list of many?

Since Ruth owns this house, and it's on the road they claimed to have lived on eight years ago, was it possible that this house was where the boys lived back then? An image suddenly flickered in my mind, something I'd seen this morning—a brief glimpse of something while perching on the counter and putting that dye on my head.

Right outside the bathroom doorframe, I'd seen pale remnants of a height measurement chart drawn on the wall upstairs. At the time, I'd thought it was odd that one of Ruth's renters would write on a wall in a house they didn't own. But what if it was Ruth's family that originally lived here?

I charged up the stairs, adrenaline surging through my veins. Flashes of what I'd seen on the wall this morning.

The lighting was poor on the second floor, so I unplugged a small desk lamp in the bedroom and brought it over close to the wall. Sure enough, the light revealed tiny scribbled lines where someone had marked their child's height, and there were names written beside each squiggly line.

I stared at the messy, faded traces of writing, trying to make out the individual letters in their names. I hated to be sexist, but I was sure it had to be a man's handwriting because it looked so messy. I squatted down on my haunches, squinting at the lines. Despite the scribbly words, I could make out three names. The shortest line said 'Zach' beside it. *Good old Zeke*, I thought, narrowing my eyes at his line.

Sure enough, the taller line belonged to James, aka Joey. I thought about that thuggish boy, the one I'd coveted as a young teen. I could remember the contours of his face so clearly. He was dead now, and I didn't feel a bit sorry for him, especially after what he and his brother did to me and Claire.

I squinted at the line drawn above his, trying to make out the name. It was 'Jennifer.' I ran the tip of my finger across each letter, certain that's what it read. I took a step back, my mind spinning. Could Jennifer possibly be my Jeanna? I rested my pointer finger on the letter 'J' in her name, my heart beating fearfully.

Chapter Thirty-Six

I sat on the couch, staring at the cheap flip phone on my lap, willing the pieces to come together in my mind. Looking over the list I'd made, there were still so many unknowns. I had to get some answers from Ruth, but the last thing I needed or wanted to do was arouse her, or her husband's, suspicions of me. I needed to handle this carefully; there could be no mistakes or else I'd be putting mine and my parents' lives in jeopardy.

I reviewed what I was going to say in my mind several times, and then I dialed the telephone number Ruth had listed on the lease agreement. I squeezed my eyes shut, praying it wouldn't be Charlie who answered. The last thing I wanted to hear was that dry, gravelly voice of his.

"Hello?" It was Ruth. *Now it's time to hone in on your acting skills*, I reminded myself anxiously.

"Hey, Ruth! I'm so sorry to bother you, but I just wanted to call and thank you again for dinner.

You've treated me with such kindness…"

"No mind, dear! We enjoyed your company! Even Charlie, and he's a quiet, old grump normally," she said jokingly.

"That's fantastic, Ruth. I truly appreciated the dinner. The food was delicious. And I'm grateful for you letting me stay here. It's truly a wonderful place."

"I'm so glad to hear it, Elsie. Is there anything else I can do for you tonight?" Ruth asked, sounding curious as to why I was calling so late.

"Mainly, this was just a courtesy call, but I did want to mention something to you about some writing on the wall in the house."

When Ruth didn't answer, I went on. "I'm not sure if it was one of your past renters, but I saw the name Jennifer on the wall by the bathroom…I couldn't read any of the other names very well, but I'm bringing it up…because I don't want you to think it was me that did the damage…I'd never write on the walls, Ruth," I promised sweetly, immensely impressed by my own acting skills.

"Oh, honey, no worries! I already knew about the writing upstairs." For a moment, I was scared she was just going to leave it at that, and hang up the phone without supplying any answers.

But then she said, "Jennifer wasn't my biological daughter, but she was basically mine. You see, I had James when I was young, with a boy I met right out of high school. After I had him, his father ran off and never built a relationship with his son. That's when I met Hank. Hank was older than me and had a teenage daughter named Jennifer. We bought a house—the house you're in now, in fact—and we started a life together. Jennifer didn't have a mom and James didn't have a dad, so we raised our children together. It was great for both of us, and James and Jennifer got along so well. Jennifer was nearly ten years older than James, but they still played together and adored one another."

There was no stopping Ruth from chattering now. "When I found out I was pregnant with Zach, it was perfect. Hank and I were raising each other's babies, and now we were having one of our own. But the house was too crowded, and we eventually bought something bigger. That's when we started renting out the house you're in now...I'm sorry, honey...here I am, telling a young girl my boring life story..."

"No, I appreciate you sharing your story with me, Ruth!" I declared, a sickening sweetness to my tone. "If you don't mind me asking, what happened to you and Hank?" I asked timidly, wondering if I was pressing my luck and raising suspicion.

"Oh, Hank and I...the only thing that kept us together was our love for the children. We eventually went our separate ways. He and Jennifer got their own place, and I moved into the house I'm in now with the boys. I'd known Charlie for years, and we eventually got together. Charlie was a friend of the family, and one of Hank's friends too."

I sat there for a moment, taking it all in. "So, they moved away? And you didn't see Jennifer anymore? I'm sure that was hard since she was your stepdaughter..."

"Oh, no! I still got to see her all the time! Hank

and Jennifer moved to their own house on Clemmons Street, which was just a few streets away. Well, I'm tired, honey…thanks for calling, and we'll get together again soon, I hope."

I thanked her again and hung up. I stared at the phone again thoughtfully. I got up, went to the kitchen, and grabbed a family-sized box of Fruit Loops. I sat back down and began eating the sugary cereal dry, digging it out with my hands.

I ate quickly, my thoughts focused intently on the new information I had. Was it possible that Jennifer and Jeanna were the same person? Could the house of horrors be the house on Clemmons Street that Ruth spoke of? I still wasn't sure who Hank was. Could he possibly be Jed, or one of the men whose faces I didn't see in those darkened rooms? I considered the possibility that maybe this Hank was not even involved in my kidnapping, but that seemed unlikely.

There was just so much for me to take in, and I was feeling overwhelmed. Maybe I was losing my mind. "Or…maybe I'm right," I considered aloud, stuffing more cereal in my mouth.

Chapter Thirty-Seven

I tossed and turned all night long, images of faceless monsters chasing me through the dark, endless streets of Flocksdale. Specifically, I dreamt of the ominous streets surrounding what was now Mac's Super Skateland. *A super-duper place indeed*, I thought angrily, rolling around in the dark.

The last thing I wanted to do when my phone alarm rang was get up and go to work. But I did anyway, and I worked with a smile plastered across my face. I'd become so good at hiding my real emotions that it was second nature to me now.

I was working the front counter today, which meant I would have to spend the day interacting with people. The early morning crowd was brutal. I rang up customers back to back for hours on end until it was nearly noon.

We had about thirty minutes before the lunch rush started. A few of my co-workers smoked cigarettes, so I decided to go try to bum one. I needed a break, and smoking was a perfect excuse. It's hard to work in the restaurant business and not smoke, I'd quickly realized since joining the McDonald's crew. Smoking was a great excuse to take a break, and everybody likes breaks, including me.

A small group of staff members were already standing outside next to the building, firing up their cigs simultaneously. I told my supervisor I was taking a five minute break and made sure my station was covered. An older worker named Melanie kindly offered me a cigarette, and I leaned against the backside of the building, sucking in deep, harmful puffs.

Hordes of customers on their lunch breaks were already pulling in the lot. Crews of construction workers and business executives alike all came to eat at McDonald's. As I eyed the parking lot, I saw a dark haired woman step out of a Jeep the color of burnt oranges. She was wearing a snappy, youthful skirt and blazer, but I could tell by the age spots on her legs as she stepped out that she was anything but young. The woman was clutching a fancy, sequined purse, and when she turned around to face the restaurant's entrance, I gasped audibly. It may have been eight years since I'd seen her, but I'd recognize my mother's face anywhere.

For what seemed like an hour, I didn't breathe or move. I stared as she approached the restaurant, unable to pull my eyes away from her face. Her movements were slow and drawn out, like I was on some acid trip.

I couldn't believe it! What luck I was having. I

couldn't let her see me. Not now, and not like this!

I wanted to see her again someday, but not until after I'd had my revenge. I wasn't ready for a reunion just yet. I quickly darted to the back of the building, peering back around the edge of the building's stucco façade, watching her approach the restaurant. My mother strutted through the front door, a serious look on her face. Her face was lined with worry and heartache. She looked as though she'd aged twenty years instead of eight since I'd last seen her. *Losing a daughter will do that you*, I thought guiltily.

My mother has been cutting hair since she was a teenager, and I'd bet she was taking a break for her lunch hour. I couldn't help thinking about the sadness in her face and eyes as she disappeared through the entrance and went inside.

I wondered about the toll that losing her only child must have had on her—and my father too. I felt sick to my stomach with guilt. I imagined myself running inside, throwing my arms around her neck. Begging her to forgive me. What a shock that would be for her!

But the truth was, revealing my identity now would spoil everything. I wasn't ready for my family to know the truth, even though I wanted to reunite with them now. I was still concerned for their safety and my own. The news of my homecoming would spread throughout the town, and would eventually reach Ruth, Zach, and their entire family. It would reach Jeanna too, who I suspected was actually Ruth's stepdaughter, Jennifer. I wanted to be with my mom. But I simply couldn't do it. It was too risky.

I hid out behind the building until I saw her get back in the Jeep and pull away, which was nearly thirty minutes later. I knew I was going to be in trouble with my supervisor for disappearing so long during the lunch rush. After gaining my composure, I finally went back inside, ready to face the music so to speak, and unable to erase the image of my mother's face from my mind.

Chapter Thirty-Eight

My boss, Andrea, was surprisingly sympathetic about my extended break. I made up some stupid story about getting sick outside. I followed her back to her stuffy, cramped office space, and I waited for her to yell at me.

But she didn't. Instead she asked, "You're not using again, are you, Elsie?" I don't know why I was so surprised to hear that question. It only made perfect sense that Mark would tell her about my past drug issues when he sent over my transfer request, but it still stung. There's just something about the stigma of being an addict; you carry it around for life. Any time you're not yourself or you make a mistake, people will always ask that question: "Are you using drugs again?" It seriously pisses me off.

"No, I'm not using drugs. I promise. But I still feel rough at times, and I do still have cravings," I told her, which was partially true.

"Why don't you take the rest of the day off?" Andrea suggested. She patted my shoulders thoughtfully.

I hated to lose out on the money, but I did have my own work to do. Not to mention the fact I was seriously shaken up from seeing my mother so abruptly after all of these years.

I headed back home, stopping again in front of the skating rink. It was a weekday afternoon, and I didn't expect it to be very busy. Surprisingly though, the parking lot was crowded with cars, and there were young families standing out front, roller skates in hand. Business must be doing well.

Taking a deep breath, I made a beeline for the door. I hadn't planned on going in, but I suddenly felt compelled to do so. The front stone entranceway looked new and fresh, but the inside was still the same. All of the paint layers in the world couldn't make me forget about this place. It wasn't the house of horrors, but it was the site of my initial abduction, and just being here induced a deep, raw fear in my gut.

There was a man perched on a stool at the door, collecting five dollar bills from kids and parents. There were nearly six people in front of me in line. What was I doing? Was I really going to pay and go inside? Would this really help my investigation?

I decided it was worth a shot. As I approached the ticket taker, I suddenly froze in terror. The old man on the stool was the same old guy that took my ticket all those years ago. It's not that I suspected his involvement in my kidnapping, but the thought of him seeing me and knowing who I was was horrifying.

I turned away before he could see me and headed back out the door. That's when I saw something even more disconcerting—a lone, grainy flier hanging at the bottom of a bulletin board in the entranceway. A picture of my face. It read in big, blockish letters:

Have You Seen This Girl?

I pulled my cap down low and slipped out of there as quickly as I could without attracting any attention.

***

I walked around to the back side of the skating rink and headed down the first street, taking the same route I'd taken that day when I was kidnapped. I could remember thinking that the houses on this street looked rough, with their clutter and covered windows. They looked basically the same as they always had. I imagined the sounds of Claire and the boys, chattering as we walked along the deserted street. I remembered the strange flutter in my stomach when I'd seen the limo approaching.

I thought about the girl in the picture. I wondered why I didn't see any pictures of Claire hanging up at the skating rink. Surely, they were still looking for her too. Did her parents somehow know she was already dead?

I wondered who was responsible for hanging up that picture of me. I tried to imagine my mother, father, or both of them walking in the skating rink, hanging up the picture, full of desperation. The picture was my sixth grade school photo, so it had to be my parents that pinned it on the bulletin board.

How many years had it been hanging there? Had my parents searched for me? Had the police looked for me too? I couldn't help but wonder if my parents were still holding out hope that I'd come back some day. The thought that they'd given up on me was too much to bear.

I cut through someone's yard, crossing over to my house on Saints Road. But instead of going home, I strolled right past the rental house, heading for the adjacent neighborhood where the man in the limo had taken Jeanna her drugs. Was Ruth's stepdaughter, Jennifer, and Jeanna the same person? I couldn't shake that thought.

I kept track of how long it took me to get to the house. It was nearly a fifteen minute walk. I wasn't sure how that compared to a ten minute drive with a blindfold on, but I still wondered if this might be the house where I'd been held.

I stood on the sidewalk in front of it, staring up at those old, stone steps that led to the two-story house. I'd been inside this house so many years ago, and it's where I'd met Jeanna for the first time. I'd sat inside, uncomfortable as hell, while Jeanna did her drugs—but never once suspected what lay ahead in my future.

I wasn't sure what I was going to do, or how it helped me to stand here in front of this house. But then I spotted a row of plastic mailboxes at the curb, and I nonchalantly strolled closer toward them.

The house number was 114, and I immediately saw the corresponding mailbox. Stealing people's mail is a federal offense, but after everything I'd been through and still planned to do, did one small crime really matter at this point? I decided that it didn't.

I looked around, trying to play it cool. Luckily, I didn't see any random dog walkers or neighbors out working in their yards, not as far as I could see. I stuck my hand in the box quickly. Nothing. It was empty. Damn the luck.

I turned to walk away, but then a voice called out, "What are you doing?" and I froze in place with fear.

Chapter Thirty-Nine

I looked up the steep staircase at the woman looking down at me. She was an elderly woman, and she looked as frail as a baby bird. I'd never seen her before in my life. "Ummm...I'm just out walking," I replied defensively.

"Oh. I saw you looking at the house, so I thought maybe you were lost or looking for someone in particular," she said with a slight smile. I wondered if she saw my hand in her mailbox and if so, was she going to confront me about it?

"Sorry. No, I'm just new to the neighborhood. I was checking out the scenery. Admiring your house. It's lovely," I said, wondering if I sounded like a phony idiot. I definitely felt like one.

I turned to walk away, thanking my lucky stars to get out of there, and for not getting called out for rifling through her mail. The woman didn't look familiar at all, and I was starting to wonder if this whole thing was a waste of time. If Jeanna had lived in that house before, she certainly didn't seem to now. This old woman was far older than Jeanna would be now.

"You said you're new to the neighborhood. Whereabouts do you live?" the woman called out, stopping me dead in my tracks.

"I live on Saints Road, in a rental house," I said honestly, turning back around to look at her.

"Ah. Ruth and Hank's old place," she said, shocking me.

"You know the house?" I asked, trying not to seem surprised. I guess it made perfect sense, really. After all, this was a small town. Everyone around here probably knows each other. *Dummy*, I scolded myself.

"Yes. I know that house well. Ruth used to be my daughter-in-law. Hank is my son, you see...he grew up right here in this house, and raised his daughter here when she was little. Small world, eh?"

If only you knew, lady, I thought with a smile. "Wow. That is amazing!" I exclaimed, being fake as hell. "Ruth was just telling me last night about Hank and his daughter, Jennifer. Is that the granddaughter you're talking about?" I inquired sweetly.

"She is!" the woman exclaimed. "I know spending time with an old woman isn't much fun, but would you like to come inside? Maybe have a glass of iced tea?" she offered politely.

"Sure," I said, following her inside. I probably should've been frightened of entering this stranger's house, but she was old and frail, after all. Surely I could defend myself against this old broad.

As soon as I walked in, I immediately recognized the front living room I'd sat in that day when Jed brought us, but the furniture had completely changed. The long sectional had been replaced with a modern couch and two matching ottomans. My eyes darted around the room nervously, making sure Jeanna wasn't inside.

I thought about Jeanna sitting there so many years ago, toking her meth-filled pipe. We passed by the sitting area, and she led me into an eat-in kitchen. This wasn't the same room where I'd dined with Jeanna on that day she let me go, and the house didn't seem large enough to be the house of horrors.

But this was somewhere Jeanna once lived, with her father and grandmother. That seemed important for some reason. Another small piece to the puzzle.

"I forgot to ask your name," I admitted embarrassingly. "It's Margie," she said, filling two tall glasses with ice.

"I'm Elsie," I said, wandering around the kitchen as she poured the tea. There weren't any pictures I could see, at least not in this room or the front sitting area. "You have a nice home. Have you lived here a long time?" I pried innocently.

"Oh, yes. The Garretts have owned this home for generations. My mother raised me in this house, and I raised Hank here. He got a girl pregnant when he was a teen, and I had to help him take care of Jennifer until he met Ruth and moved in with her and her son," she said, traces of bitterness in her tone.

The tea was sugarless, and my mouth blanched. I forced myself to swallow the watery, flavorless substance. "Did you say your last name was Garrett?" I asked, pushing the drink aside. "Yes, that was my father's name and it became mine and my son's," Margie proclaimed proudly.

I thought about the man who was with Jeanna all the time, overseeing things. I heard her and a couple others refer to him as 'Garrett' on several occasions. He'd looked older than Jeanna, but not old enough to be her father. But I pondered over Margie's story. If Hank Garrett was a teenage father, then that would explain the narrow age difference. It would also explain why I'd thought 'Garrett' was Jeanna's boyfriend, since they looked so close in age, and both seemed to be running the show.

I had no doubt now: Garrett and Jeanna were the same as Hank and Jennifer. I could feel it in my bones. Margie stood with her back to me, washing out her cup in the sink. I wondered if she knew what her son and granddaughter had been up to. I wondered if she was involved. That brought me around to my next question: my landlord Ruth had been Hank's wife and Jennifer's stepmother. Ruth had also been the mother of the two boys that lured us to the house of horrors. How could she not be involved too?

They're all guilty, I realized, standing up from the table. Margie stood facing the kitchen counter, filling her glass with more tea. Her back was to me, and I stood so close to her I was surprised she didn't feel me breathing down her neck. She was so old and fragile; all I had to do was wrap my hands around her neck and I could squeeze the life out of her with ease. God knows I had enough pent up rage to go through with it.

But it's not time yet, I decided. I didn't have all the answers yet, and maybe I never would. But I needed more certainty before I acted out, and before I harmed an elderly woman. "Thanks for the drink. Nice to meet you," I said, heading for the door.

Chapter Forty

As soon as I was out of Margie's field of vision, I took off down the sidewalk, sprinting. I ran until my lungs felt like they were going to burst and my side ached painfully. The afternoon sun drifted behind the clouds. A storm was coming in. *A real storm and a metaphorical one*, I thought bitterly. By the time I stopped running, I was wheezing slightly.

I slowed down to a walk and started making my way toward Ruth's house on Merribeth Avenue. I wasn't going to her house, but I was going somewhere close. Ruth said that her youngest son lived on Weston Street, and I had to see with my own eyes if Zach was actually the boy, Zeke, from my youth. If given the chance, I wouldn't hesitate to snap his neck.

Thinking about those boys' trickery and all of the adults who were involved in hurting me and ultimately killing Claire, I felt so angry that I was seriously homicidal. But I wasn't sure if my thoughts could really be translated into action. I'd never physically harmed another person in my life.

175

It reminded me of the psychiatric aides at the rehab clinic, always asking me and the other patients there if we were suicidal or homicidal. *Like we'd really tell them if we were.*

I rounded the corner of Hampton Street, looking for more street signs. Specifically, I was looking for Clemmons and Weston Street. When I spoke on the phone to Ruth the other night, she'd revealed that Hank and Jennifer had eventually moved to a house on Clemmons Street. But I wasn't sure where that was. I wondered if it was somewhere nearby. I sensed that it was.

There was something about this entire town that quickened my pulse and made me uneasy. It was like there was this inexplicable eeriness in the air, an invisible cloud of evil surrounding me, pressing down on my chest and making it hard to breathe.

Pellets of rain were starting to fall, but I ignored the wetness and the chill. The icy drops felt great on my raging hot skin. Weston Street was nearly five streets back from Ruth's house. By the time I made it there, it was pouring. I didn't give a damn if I was getting soaked, or if anyone saw me scoping out the neighborhood.

I could see heavy puffs of smoke in the distance, pouring out of a grey factory on the other side of a river. I wondered if that was where Zach worked, but then I remembered Ruth saying her son was a plumber. I wasn't sure what kind of hours plumbers worked, or if he would even be home. I wasn't even sure about the house number. All I knew was that he lived on Weston Street. I was hoping that Clemmons Street was nearby too.

The houses on Weston Street were quiet and dark, with most of its occupants gone to work for the day, presumably. Even though it was still daylight, the cloudy skies created the illusion of nightfall. I crept down the street slowly, trying not to look suspicious, but also taking my time and being observant.

A few of the houses had names displayed in the front: The Johnsons and The Carpenters. But I didn't see any signs that said Garrett, and I saw no signs of Zach. I was seriously considering opening mailboxes again when I saw something that made my blood run cold. Parked behind one of the houses, pulled beneath a carport and under a rust-stained tarp was the unmistakable shape of that hideous limousine.

Chapter Forty-One

I took off running frantically, darting through people's yards. I don't know why, but I was suddenly fearful, and I imagined that monstrous limo, charging down the black, deserted streets behind me. I was convinced it was chasing me home, but by the time I made it to my house on Saints Road, the streets were empty.

I let myself in and collapsed onto the couch, pulling my green comforter up to my chin. I shivered uncontrollably. I was terrified. What was I doing back in Flocksdale? If they found out, I was dead for sure. There was no way they would let me get away a second time.

My clothes were soaked, but I didn't care. I hid under the covers like a scared child, and bawled into the couch cushions until they were saturated with my tears.

Rain drops were beating down on the roof and I could hear howls of the wind in the distance. A loud clap of thunder made me jump, and then suddenly, the power went out. I sat there, frozen in terror, not sure what to do.

I didn't have any flashlights or candles in the house to provide light. I sat there, perfectly still for hours, listening for sounds in the dark, convinced that someone was coming for me. I even went so far as to creep over to the window and peer down the street, making sure no one was actually out there, hiding in the darkness.

The fear I felt deep inside reminded me of those horrific experiences when I was taking meth. There were so many nights when I'd sat home alone, afraid of every sight and sound, and seeing things that weren't really there.

But this time, my fears were real and warranted. I had every reason to be afraid. It wasn't just the house of horrors that frightened me; it was the entire town of Flocksdale, filled with horrible, depraved people.

For a moment, lying there in the dark, I imagined I was back in the house of horrors. The sights and sounds of it invaded my senses, making it hard to breathe. I was on my couch, but I was there too, smelling their sweaty skin and feeling their flabby skin touching mine as I lay in the darkness.

"You're so soft," said a voice in my ear. It was Charlie. I leapt to my feet, running through the house, trying to escape my stress-induced hallucination. I fiddled around in the dark until I'd found the front door. I burst through it, sucking in deep gulps of cold air, bent over at the waist on my porch.

I knew it was all in my head. Charlie wasn't in my house. But the flashback had felt so real, and I now knew beyond a shadow of a doubt that Charlie was, in fact, one of those men in that horrific house.

I sat outside for an hour, my only light coming from the moon. It was full and luminous, a giant disk in the sky providing me cool relief from my dark fears. I chain smoked, rocking back and forth until I felt okay again. Finally, at nearly midnight, I crept inside and laid on the couch. The power was still out, but I was too tired to care.

My dreams were riddled with frightening images. Claire's face morphing into my mother's, and the picture with the words, 'Have You Seen This Girl?', only the face on it was distorted, changing into images of people that looked vaguely familiar, but not. I imagined that limo speeding down the roads of Flocksdale, Jeanna laughing maniacally behind the wheel.

Chapter Forty-Two

When I woke up the next morning, the lights were back on and the sun was shining warmly through the flimsy curtains that covered them. I got up from the couch begrudgingly. My body ached from the previous fear-filled night.

I slipped on my work clothes and ran a comb through my hair. On the walk to work, I felt tired and depressed. But then, out of nowhere, I was hit with a brilliant idea. I picked up the pace, humming the whole way to work.

***

McDonald's offered free Wi-Fi, and even though I didn't own a computer, my coworker let me borrow her laptop on my lunch break. I told her I was applying for college and needed to do some research. *What a stupid lie*, I thought, pulling up a popular search engine, and edging my chair closer to the table.

I looked around nervously, making sure no one was behind me or close enough to see what I was doing. I entered the words, 'Wendi Wise' and 'missing' and 'Flocksdale' in the search engine's empty space. I waited.

Suddenly, I was bombarded with images of grainy newspaper articles. My parents were on the front page, their faces twisted and contorted into painful masks, begging the public for information. At first, the police worried that I'd been kidnapped, and questions about possible motives and ransom demands were thrown around in the articles. But later articles revealed speculative reports of me being a runaway. Again, more pleading from my mom and dad, asking me to please come home. There was even a short blurb in one of the articles about my recent troubles with shoplifting and lying to my parents.

At first, I was this poor, innocent girl who was ripped away from her parents unjustly, but then I was painted as a troubled youth, who no one was surprised to find missing. I wanted to kill whoever wrote these shitty articles. I couldn't imagine my parents' reaction. Did they really believe I was a runaway? Did they really think I would just up and leave them, regardless of what sort of trouble I was in? Did they consider me to be "troubled," like the papers claimed? It broke my heart to consider it.

"Have You Seen This Girl?" it said at the top of one article, and it featured the same school picture I'd seen on the flier at the skating rink. I stared at my own face in the picture. I hadn't seen that innocent girl in a very long time. Not even when I looked in the mirror. She really was gone. Just not in the way everyone thought.

There were dozens of photographs of me, more school pictures that were awkward and old. Surely, no one could recognize me, even if they saw the missing poster or these images…or would they? All of the articles were at least five or more years old; I'd grown and changed since then, and the townspeople had probably forgotten after the initial excitement of my disappearance died down.

I was worried that someone in the restaurant might peer over my shoulder and see my face online, so I quickly X'ed out all of the screens, deleted the search history, and closed the laptop noisily.

"Thanks," I said, walking back behind the line, handing the laptop to the girl who let me borrow it. Strangely, her name was Sunshine, and ironically, she was always beaming from ear to ear.

"Oh, you're welcome! Did you find some great colleges?" she asked gleefully.

"Changed my mind," I said, heading back to my work station.

***

I was still waiting on my first paycheck from this new location, but I had some money left over from my partial deposit. After work, I went to the drugstore across the street and perused the aisles, looking for something in particular.

I finally found a small flashlight and a package

of cheap tea light candles. I didn't want to get stuck in the dark again, not if I could help it. I also found a small boombox on one of the shelves. It wasn't as nice or big as the one I'd had before, but it would work just fine.

***

By the time I left the store with my boom box and flashlight stuff in hand, it was nearly dark outside. I walked home, taking my time and enjoying the fresh, cool air. There was a gentle breeze floating up from the river, and despite my hatred of this town, I had to admit that the weather here beat the weather in Albuquerque any day of the week.

I let myself inside the rental house, still joyfully humming a song. I was in a terrific mood. I had a quick bite to eat, and then I dialed Ruth's number. She answered on the first ring.

"Hi, Elsie! Is everything going okay?"

"Well, actually, I have a problem. My toilet overflowed on the bathroom floor and I can't get it unclogged. Getting a plumber out this late may prove to be impossible. But you said your son, Zach, was a plumber, right? Is there any way you can send him over here to help me?"

Chapter Forty-Three

I was strangely calm as I waited for him to arrive. Ruth hung up with me, and then called me back, to inform me that Zach was on his way. It would take him a while to get here, she said, because he was coming on foot.

Like Claire and I, Zach and James were children at the time all of this happened. In truth, the young boys probably weren't to blame. But I honestly didn't care. I still held them responsible for the role they played in hurting my friend, and for hurting me too, of course.

I imagined Zach's face, pudgy with a little bit of fuzz, smiling at my best friend, conning her all along. Zach's actions ultimately led to the death of my friend, and for that, I blamed him wholeheartedly.

I stood in the kitchen, calmly eating Salisbury steaks straight out of the package they'd come in, staring out the window at the bluish-black night sky. I'd just finished my last bite when I heard a knock at the door. I opened it without hesitation.

A heavyset, older version of Zeke/Zach stood on my front porch, carrying a chunky bag of tools. He didn't look as scary as I'd imagined, not even standing out there in the pitch dark. "Come in," I said, avoiding eye contact as much as possible. "The problem is upstairs. Your mom said you used to live here, so you know where the toilet is, right?"

"I know where it's at," he answered quietly, heading straight for the stairs. He seemed different, shyer, and he barely even glanced at me. He was dressed in dark jeans and heavy boots. I watched him walk up the stairs, burning holes into his backside with my eyes.

Instead of following him, I slipped down the stairs into the earthy-smelling basement. The knives were displayed on a cardboard box, along with my brand new boombox. It was show time. I pressed play on the CD and immediately, a familiar, haunting tune filled the cavernous space. I turned up the volume as high as it would go, and then I flipped off the main breaker to the house.

The power outage last night was terrifying, but it had inspired me. The house was now filled with darkness, and in my hand, I felt the rubbery handle of the knife.

Chapter Forty-Four

I walked stealthily, creeping slowly for two reasons: I didn't want Zach to hear me coming, and I also didn't want to fall and break my neck in the dark. I walked up the basement steps, the sounds of the music thumping, rocking my very soul. The familiar lyrics of Jim Morrison resounded through my head and reverberated in my chest. It was a song I'd never forget.

Despite the horror I'd originally associated with the song, its words held a new meaning for me now. It was the end of me initially, but now it was the end of *them*, the monsters who had kidnapped me and stolen my best friend's life. Wendi Wise was back. I was ready to take them on and put an end to the misery they'd caused me and so many others for so many years...

Zach hadn't moved a muscle or called out in the dark, or if he had, I hadn't heard him. I crept upstairs, feeling my way along the walls through the darkness, heading toward the small bathroom above.

I reached the top of the stairs, moving as quietly as possible. I took nearly ten steps forward, moving blindly in the dark. I held the knife at my side.

"Sir, are you in there? I don't know what happened!" I called out, my voice trembling.

"I'm right here," said a deep voice behind me. I pulled a small flashlight from my back pocket and flipped it on, just in time to see him creeping toward me. The song said it all, and I was certain that he knew who I was, standing there with him in the darkness.

He was right in front of me now, stepping forward cautiously. My eyes adjusted to the blackness, and I was suddenly hit with a strange sense of inner calmness. He was so close I could smell his body odor and stale breath. It was time.

He was right in front of me now, and we stood face-to-face, staring at each other knowingly. But there was one thing he didn't know or realize: I was holding a knife.

Without warning, I lifted the weapon, stepped forward, and plunged the knife deep in his chest. He let out a strange, breathless attempt at a scream. "I really did like you," I whispered in his ear as I shoved the knife deeper into his soft flesh. That night in the house of horrors, I'd thought it was James whispering those words to me. "I really liked you," the voice said...but last night I'd realized whose voice it really was saying them. It was Zach. I think I'd known it all along.

Chapter Forty-Five

The flashlight didn't provide much illumination in the velvety blackness. What made me think this was a good idea, stabbing at him in the dark? He let out a small *oomph* when I pushed the knife in farther, and then we fell to the floor together. I was on top of him. He lay slumped beneath me on the floor, noiselessly.

My hand was still gripping the handle of the knife shakily. I wanted to stab him again and again, but I couldn't get the knife out of his chest. It was lodged in a soft spot over his right breast. Blood spread out around the knife, soaking his pale yellow Polo. I yanked on the knife with all my might, but it wouldn't budge from his chest. Zach made pitiful moaning sounds and jerked from side to side, trying to knock me off him.

The dull glow of the flashlight provided little help in the dark. I could barely see what I was doing, and my attempts at pulling out the knife were futile.

I made a quick decision. Leaving him lying there, I ran downstairs to turn the main breaker switch back on. I was certain he was dead or dying, but I had to make sure. The song was still playing, eerie words about riding a snake and the end of nights people tried to die…

I raced down the cellar stairs. On the second or third stair, my foot abruptly slipped out from under me. I went tumbling to the bottom, scraping my back all the way down. I panted and groaned, pulling myself back up to my feet. I didn't have a flashlight or any source of light, so I spun around aimlessly in the dark, trying to find the wall with the breaker box.

I felt like I was going to hyperventilate, but somehow, someway, I traced my hands along the wall until I found that dreadful box, and I found the one left-sided switch. The power roared back to life like a godsend. I let out a deep whoosh of breath.

I took off running back up the stairs. I turned the corner, and that's when I saw the bloody mess on the carpet. A dark, crimson stain, as large and wide as a person. But Zach's body was nowhere near the bloody puddle. He had somehow managed to get away!

Chapter Forty-Six

It didn't make sense. How could his body just disappear? There were no doors leading outside from up here, and I would have heard him if he'd come down the stairs…wouldn't I?

I crept toward the lightless bathroom, wondering if he'd pulled himself inside it, and maybe he was still alive. Maybe he was just wounded, waiting to attack me. That's when he charged straight at me, running out from the back corner of the bathroom, and knocking the wind out of me as I tumbled backwards. I grabbed onto the towel bar as I went down, trying to break my fall, and it collapsed to the ground with me.

He ran at me like a wild bull covered in blood, with the knife still lodged in his chest. Unlike him, I wasn't injured, so I moved more speedily, jumping up with the towel bar in hand. Now that I was back on my feet, I poked at him with the lousy towel bar, backing up desperately. He chuckled at me

191

maniacally.

"I lied. I never liked you, Wendi," he said, grabbing for me. I stepped back, but he charged again. I moved quickly, and just in time. He fell forward, banging his head on the heavy metal radiator that stood outside the bathroom door. He crumpled to the floor beside it, his body lifeless.

I crept forward, edging toward him on my tip-toes, fear surging through my entire body. What if he was pretending? I held that stupid towel bar out in front of me, protectively, and I moved as close to him as I dared. I leaned down and felt his pulse. He was still alive!

I ran downstairs, grabbing a long, twisted rope that was hanging on a hook in the cellar. I dragged the heavy rope back upstairs with me. He was breathing, but unconscious. I had to seize the moment. I began tying his arms to the radiator, trying to finish before he woke up and tried to kill me again.

Chapter Forty-Seven

I sat on the living room couch, chewing on my fingernails until they were sore and bleeding. Who had I become? What was I going to do with him now that I had him tied up? Even if he died up there, I had to dispose of the body. What the hell was I thinking when I concocted this crazy plan?

I'd closed the door to the upstairs. Shoved one of the metal chairs up under the knob. So, even if he broke free from the ropes, he would still have to struggle at the door long enough to alert me.

When I get my paycheck, I could buy a gun and shoot him in the head, I considered, chewing on the bloody nails relentlessly. *But...then what? He was too big to move. Maybe I could slide his body inside the bathroom.*

The only way to get rid of his body would be to chop him into pieces. I could buy a Sawzall...I shuddered at the thought, my stomach lurching. I felt like I needed to throw up, but I couldn't use my own bathroom because a half dead guy was waiting upstairs for me.

An image of me chopping through his flesh, bone dust flying through the air around me, entered my mind...I ran over to the garbage can and promptly vomited in it.

Wiping my mouth, I pulled the bag out of the can, and carried it outside to the city can in the desolate backyard. That was my only liner until payday, I realized miserably. The fact that I could worry about everyday household concerns at a time like this frightened me. Was I as bad as them?

I walked inside the house and fell back onto the couch. I covered my head with the blanket again and closed my eyes. I thought about the way it felt when the knife ruptured his skin, shaking with disgust and fear. I never should have done this. Never, never, never...

I was physically and mentally done for the day. I don't know how I did it, but I drifted off into a dreamless sleep, snoring away on the couch...

Chapter Forty-Eight

I woke up two hours later, at quarter after one in the morning. It was the sounds of groaning upstairs that awoke me. I groaned myself, standing up from the couch. My right arm felt heavy and sore. *Probably because you stabbed someone with it*, I thought guiltily.

I crept up the stairs and pressed my ear to the door.

"I know you're there," Zach grumbled creepily from somewhere on the other side of the door. I gasped, nearly falling backwards down the stairs. "Please untie me and I'll explain everything," he whined, a surprisingly babyish tone to his voice.

So, he was still tied up at least, I realized, crossing my arms smugly. "There's nothing to talk about. I'm going to kill you," I hissed through the door.

"But it wasn't my fault. It really wasn't," he moaned pathetically.

I pulled the chair out from under the knob and threw open the door angrily. I stomped over to where he was lying on the floor tied up, and kicked him promptly in the face. My foot connected with his nose and his head snapped back. I enjoyed the sound of it. I was hoping to knock him out cold again, but he was regrettably still conscious. His mouth and nose were bleeding.

He spat the blood on the carpet, snarling up at me. "Even if you kill me and somehow destroy my body, you'll never be able to explain all this blood on the floor. My mom is going to freak," he said, looking around the room wildly. I wanted to kick him again, but what he said sort of rang true. Ruth would eventually come looking for her son, the plumber. She knew he was here, and it wouldn't be long before she started wondering where he was.

"If you tell me everything I want to know, then I'll consider letting you go," I told him honestly. I wondered if what I was saying were true; I wasn't so sure myself. I doubted that simply letting him go was even an option at this point. "Wait a minute," I said. I ran downstairs and grabbed a pack of cigarettes and lighter from my backpack. I brought them back upstairs with me.

"Can I have one of those?" Zach asked, staring at me with big doe eyes.

"You're kidding, right?" I asked, taking a relieving puff for myself.

"If you give me one, I'll tell you everything," he pleaded desperately.

"If you want to *live*, you'll tell me everything. Get your priorities straight, Zach. Or should I call you Zeke, since that's what you like to go by with the ladies?" I asked bitterly.

He stared at the burning cigarette longingly, but I wasn't budging. This asshole deserved no pleasures in life. I certainly had no pleasure when I was held captive in the house of horrors.

I sat there smoking in silence, staring at his blood on the floor. Waiting for him to talk. "Ruth is my mom. She was James' mom too. But James is dead now. His stupid, drunken ass fell off the side of a roof while we were laying shingles. We were half-brothers. My father's name is Hank. I also have a half-sister, Jennifer."

"And Jennifer and Hank are the ones who were in charge," I said, bored with hearing information I already knew.

"Not exactly," he said.

"What do you mean, not exactly? Stop yanking my chain," I shouted, stubbing out the cigarette on the floor. There was no point worrying about the carpet anymore, that much I knew for sure.

"You don't even know, do ya?" he taunted, a smug smile on his face. *I can't wait to knock that look off his face again*, I thought crossly. But then my thoughts were interrupted by the sounds of loud, thunderous bangs on the front door below.

I froze, my feet rooted to the floor momentarily. *Who in the world would be knocking at my door at nearly two in the morning?* I wondered incredulously. But then it became obvious. It had to be Ruth. When she didn't hear back from me or Zach regarding the plumbing issue, she must have worried something was wrong. I didn't know what to do.

"You're gonna die," Zach snarled menacingly. I kicked him again in the face, but this time I put more force behind it.

"You bitch!" he screamed, spitting out one of his canine teeth.

"Who's the bitch now?" I asked, winking down at him.

The banging downstairs continued. I crept down the staircase silently, unsure what I should do. If it was Ruth, I couldn't answer the door. But how could I not when she knew I was in here?

I slowly tip-toed across the living room. Luckily, all of the drapes and blinds were snugly closed. I stood in front of the door, taking deep, fearful breaths, and then I stood on my tip-toes, peering out through the peephole while sucking in my breath. Of all the people I expected to see, this person certainly wasn't one of them. I jumped back from the door, completed stunned by the person standing on my front porch. It was Officer Milby.

Chapter Forty-Nine

Officer Milby had come all of the way from Albuquerque, and here he was, standing on my front porch in Flocksdale. How the hell had he found me? And what was he doing here exactly?

I leaned against the door, pressing my back against it, completely in shock from the day's events. What the hell was going on?

Officer Milby started banging again, and I jumped back from the door, startled. "Let me in, Wendi! I know you're in there!" he shouted through the door. At the mention of my real name, I remembered that day in the parking lot at LOHP, him calling me Wendi as I ran away. Remy had told him everything, and now he'd finally found me.

"If you don't open the door, I'm going to come in anyway. God knows, I have enough probable cause, Wendi!" he warned. I stood there, wide eyed, unsure what my next move was. What choice did I have at this point?

Officer Milby started counting down. "One, two, three…" I threw open the door on four, and stepped so close to him that we were nearly nose to nose. I considered running past him, into the street beyond, but where was I going to go this time? I would rather be here, dealing with the police, than out there dealing with the maniacs of this town, I decided finally.

I stepped aside and let Officer Milby enter the house. He stepped in the living room, and now that we were standing in the light, he looked me up and down with a horrified expression on his face. What was he staring at?

I glanced down at my clothes, appalled to see that I was covered in Zach's blood. Moments earlier, I'd been snoozing away with his blood all over me, I realized with disgust.

"What's going on?" he asked, placing a hand on his gun and stepping back from me hesitantly.

Before I could explain, Zach started shouting upstairs. "Please help! She's holding me prisoner! And she said there's a body buried in the cellar, and it's one of her friends!" he screamed.

My head started spinning and I fell to my knees dizzily. Zach's words hung in the air, resonating through my head in violent, rhythmic thrusts. Why would Zach say that? And mostly, why would he say that my friend's body was down in the cellar of this house? That's when it hit me—the awful truth. Not only had Zach and his family victimized me horribly, but now they were going to pin Claire's murder on me.

Chapter Fifty

It was at that moment I realized I was going to jail. Maybe this had been my destiny all along. Hell, maybe in some way, I actually deserved this type of ending, a voice down deep inside of me was saying.

Officer Milby placed me in cuffs and sat me down on the couch. He went upstairs to assess Zach's wounds. After what seemed like an eternity, he came downstairs, covered in blood himself.

"He's lying," I started to say, but he put up a hand to stop me.

"I stopped his bleeding. Paramedics are on their way."

"But, you can't just let him go! He and his family raped me and they killed my best friend, Claire!"

"Claire. You mean the body that's supposedly in the basement of the house that *you* are renting?" Officer Milby asked, staring at me so intensely that I felt afraid of him for the first time in my life.

"I don't know anything about that! I had no idea where her body was all this time!" I screamed, tears

201

streaming down my red, hot cheeks.

I imagined Claire's gorgeous face with all its freckles and innocence, and then I pictured it again, only this time it was bloody and mangled. I imagined her dead, rotting flesh lying beneath the earthy floor of my cellar. I fought back the urge to vomit again.

But then I remembered something important, something that would clear my name. "The fingerprints! I have Jeanna's fingerprints! Her real name is actually Jennifer though...but I do have them!" I exclaimed, remembering the evidence I'd been toting around with me for years.

"What fingerprints?" he asked, raising his eyebrows skeptically.

"In the pack!" I yelled, jerking my arms around in the cuffs, trying to show him where it was located. He walked over to the backpack and unzipped it, reaching down inside.

He held up the Ziploc bag and said, "What am I supposed to do with these?"

"Those are her fingerprints. On the tape! And there's a CD downstairs in the boombox. It should still have prints on it too! They are the prints of the woman who held me prisoner," I tried to explain breathlessly. I suddenly felt like a fool and I knew what he was going to say next.

"I don't know where these prints came from. I didn't find them at a crime scene. You can't just take someone's prints and then tell me *you* found them at a crime scene. You could have easily taken these prints from anyone or taken prints off something that someone touched. This doesn't help me, Wendi. Even if these are someone's prints—a very bad person's prints—it all means nothing if I can't link it to a crime," he said, exasperated, sitting down on the couch beside me.

My heart sank. Everything he said was true, and I looked guilty as sin. "Your buddy from the rehab clinic told me your story," he said quietly.

"I know," I said, staring down at the floor miserably. I could hear ambulance sirens in the distance.

"At first, I thought it was just a story. But I've always cared about you, Wendi, and I started doing a little digging. I looked into the town of Flocksdale, and I came across the picture of a missing girl…" I squeezed my eyes shut.

"The girl in the picture was you," he finished.

I looked at him, my eyes widening. Snot slid down from my nose into my mouth. I had no free hands to wipe it away.

He pulled a picture out of his back pocket. "Have you seen this girl?" he asked, holding up the same picture of me that I saw at the skating rink. I held my breath. Was it possible that he actually thought my story was true, then? "I believe you," he said, staring back at me gravely. I let out a whoosh, my entire body filled with relief.

Chapter Fifty-One

"Stay here and don't move," Officer Milby ordered me sternly. I nodded my head, staring down at the silver cuffs on my wrists. He'd loosened them now, and I was free to move my feet at least. *He obviously trusts me*, I realized, feeling a glimmer of hope. The thought of someone knowing my story, believing it, and being in a position to help me do something about it felt overwhelmingly wonderful.

Officer Milby stood up and walked outside, probably meeting the ambulance drivers. Seconds turned into minutes, and I wondered if something was wrong. No sounds were coming from Zach upstairs, and for that, I was grateful. *I should've murdered that bastard when I had the chance*, I realized.

As much as I used to have a crush on Officer Milby, and despite the fact that he said he believed me, he was the last person I'd wanted to see right now. He'd spoiled my plans. Officer Milby was a sworn officer, and he had to operate within the parameters of the law. What I'd been doing on my own was anything but that. I was holding a man captive and I'd nearly killed him. Not to mention the aforementioned dead body in the cellar of the house I was renting.

I lifted the cuffs up to my face, trying to bite at my fingernails again. Suddenly, the door flung open and Officer Milby came barging back in. He grabbed the one metal chair that was left at the table, and he slammed it down in front of me. The look on his face was deadly serious and I sat up straighter, my back stiffening with fear.

When he took a seat, we were nose to nose. I could smell that cologne of his, and something that smelled like peppermint mouthwash. We sat there for a few seconds, staring at each other, embracing the awkward silence in the room. "Where are the paramedics?" I croaked, my throat scratchy from screaming and fighting with Zach.

"I sent them away. I told them it was a false alarm. I told them you thought you were having a heart attack, but it turned out to be a panic episode."

"But I didn't hear any sirens in the driveway," I protested, still in disbelief.

"I called them on my radio to save them the trip," he explained matter-of-factly.

"But what about him?" I asked, pointing my chin toward the upstairs doorway.

"I have a first aid kit in my cruiser and some other medical supplies. I'm going to fix him up myself," he said calmly. I stared at him like he was a werewolf from outer space.

"Did you see the knife in his chest?" I asked, shaking my head in disbelief.

"If you'd stabbed him in the heart, he would be dead by now. The blade is closer to his shoulder than his heart," he said. It sounded like an insult. I tried not to take offense.

"You're still going to have to take the knife out. He'll bleed to death without a doctor to plug the wound and fix it," I cried out desperately.

"So I guess you were planning on taking him to the doctor then, were ya?" he asked, standing up from the chair and looking at me haughtily.

"No. I was going to let him die," I answered honestly.

He stared at me with a hardened expression, his hands resting steadily on his hips. He was dressed in a pair of faded blue jeans and a casual polo. I wondered why he was here out of uniform. "What are we going to do?" I pressed.

"You don't know me as well as you think you do. Before I became a police officer, I was a first year med student at Brown. It broke my parents' hearts when I joined the force." With that, he walked back outside and came back in carrying a large first aid kit and a makeshift medical bag.

"Good luck," I said, staring down at my hands.

"Oh, you're not getting off that easily. You got me into this mess and now you're going to help me."

Chapter Fifty-Two

I sat on the floor beside Zach's outstretched body, my hands cuff-free and covered with plastic gloves. "Place your hands around the knife and apply pressure. I'm going to pull it out," Officer Milby said, staring at me fixedly.

He was sitting on his knees, leaning over Zach's other side. Zach's ropes were now replaced with shackles, and he had a gag in his mouth. Despite the horrific things he'd done, I couldn't help feeling inhumane. The tortured becomes the torturer...I didn't like being on either end.

I took a deep breath. Placed my hands around the bloody knife wound, just as I'd been instructed. Officer Milby gripped the knife. "I'm going to count to three..." he said, focusing on the wound. Zach was conscious and his eyes were wide with fear. I wondered if his fear was comparable, or possibly worse than the fear I'd felt when I was strapped down myself in that horrible room in the house of horrors. *At least he didn't watch his friend die*, I thought indignantly, as I heard Officer Milby reach "three."

He jerked the knife out of Zach's chest, pulling it out cleanly in one steady thrust. Blood flowed over onto my hands, but I held them still, awaiting Officer Milby's instructions. He began shoving what appeared to be tampons inside the man's chest. He worked quietly and methodically, despite Zach's jerky movements and agonizing wails through the gag.

As quickly as Officer Milby had pulled out the knife, he was finished filling his chest. He cleaned the area with antiseptic wipes and covered it in heavy gauze and tape. By this point, Zach had seemingly passed out from the pain. I was relieved, unable to endure anymore of his muffled cries.

Officer Milby leaned over Zach, checking his vitals. He also treated the minor wounds to his face. "Did you kick him?" he asked, covering the cuts with tiny bandages.

"Nope," I said adamantly. I was standing up now, staring down at Zach, wondering if he was as monstrous as I'd previously believed. Right now he looked pitiful, sleeping peacefully. It was hard to believe he'd played a role in the horrors of my childhood.

After Officer Milby was done treating the wounds, he looked up at me blankly. "You'll admit to stabbing the man, but not kicking him in the face?" I couldn't help it; I burst into a strange fit of inappropriate laughter. I wouldn't swear to it, but I thought I saw Officer Milby smile too.

"How did you find me?" I asked. Officer Milby rolled his eyes and stared at me pointedly. "Mark," I answered for him. I should have known.

"He didn't even ask my first name. I just told him I was family and needed to send you a birthday card."

"I have another question," I said seriously. He raised his brows.

"Why do you keep tampons in your car? Are you worried you'll get your period? And is that why you're always in a bad mood?" I joked, unable to contain my laughter anymore.

"Now you're pushing your luck," he warned, grinning at me warmly. "Let's let him sleep. You and I need to talk downstairs."

"You're not going to cuff me again?" I teased.

"Not yet," he said, looking at me with a serious expression. "I need you tell me everything. Hold nothing back," he warned. His stern voice and expression brought back memories of my father.

So, I did what Officer Milby asked me to. I told him the truth. All of it. Every last painful detail. It was the most honest conversation I'd had with anyone in my entire life.

Chapter Fifty-Three

Telling Officer Milby the truth was a huge relief. I still had that steel ball of shame and trauma around my neck, but it got a little lighter that day. "I know you were scared, but why didn't you at least tell me when you had the chance?" Officer Milby asked, pacing back and forth in front of me as I sat on the couch. I ran my fingers through my grimy hair, wishing I could take a shower instead of enduring Officer Milby's grilling session.

"Because you're the police. Duh," I answered brazenly. He stopped pacing and looked at me sternly.

"You're bull-headed, Wendi. I would have gone to bat for you. I would have figured this out without you having to take such extreme measures."

"You're going to bat for me now," I pointed out. I don't know why I was acting like such a brat, but I felt safe with this man, and I was being as honest as honest could get. I wanted him to help me. I needed him to help me.

"Yeah, I am going to help you, Wendi. But I'll probably lose my job because of it. I'm not in Flocksdale on official business. I took time off to come down here and chase after you because I was worried about you," he admitted softly, his face reddening with shame. My heart suddenly became soft as butter, seeing him be vulnerable for the first time since I'd met him.

I looked at his everyday, casual clothes and realized he was really here just for me. "Thank you," I said. I got up and walked toward him. He looked uncomfortable when I got close, and he took off for the kitchen. He opened the refrigerator and bent down, peering inside dejectedly.

"You don't have any beer? I could really use a drink," he muttered, slamming it shut.

"I'm trying to stay sober, remember?" I teased.

His expression changed as he seemed to remember my past troubles.

"Sorry," he said, turning around to face me. "And are you? Clean, I mean…" he asked, clearing his throat uncomfortably. I took another step toward him.

"I am," I said, placing my hands on his chest.

We were standing nose to nose again, but this time he didn't back away. I let my hands rest there on his chest, enjoying the feel of his chest muscles through his shirt. There was this strange static, a pleasant sort of tension, between us. I didn't want to shy away from it.

But then he turned back toward the counter and the moment was broken. He said, "The reason I didn't let him go to the hospital, and the reason I didn't contact the local police, besides the fact that you look totally guilty, is because I'm leery of whom we can trust. If all this stuff you're telling me is true, and I believe it is, we may be dealing with more than a couple evil boys and a depraved woman."

"What do you mean exactly?" I asked, leaning against the counter beside him.

"I told you I looked into your story, and I found the missing report with your picture…Well, that's not everything I found. Apparently, there's a whole lot of young girls missing from this area. After hearing all the details tonight, I'm certain there's some sort of serious trafficking ring, and influential people, such as the local police, who could possibly be involved."

I considered what he was saying. "The skating rink?" I asked, chewing on my lower lip thoughtfully.

"Possibly," he said, nodding his head. "It's one of the places where this whole thing started. Or someone recruiting people from the plaza…After meeting those boys at those places, you were taken. It would be a perfect cover for something like that, but lots of people would have to be involved," he added.

"The way you talk, it's like you think there's some type of conspiracy going on around here. But that seems a little farfetched, even after everything I've been through," I told him, chewing on my lip thoughtfully.

"Well, something has to be going on. That many

missing girls and nobody's done anything about it. They haven't called in the FBI and there are few details in the investigative reports I examined."

"So, what do we do now?" I asked.

"Well, the first thing we need to do is get my police cruiser out of your driveway. I want to drive it up to a nearby hotel, go in and rent a room for a few days, and leave it parked outside." The thought of him staying in a hotel, distanced from me, brought back that fear in my chest.

He must have realized what I was thinking because he took me by the elbow and said, "No, I'm not really going to stay at the hotel. I just don't want to alert your neighbors or any of the other townsfolk. A police car in your driveway would be like a shiny, red flag. I'm going to stay here with you and we're going to get this figured out together, and quickly. So, get your shoes on. We'll discuss some ground rules and map out your story for Ruth on the way to the hotel."

"Story for Ruth?" I asked, mesmerized by the hand still holding my elbow.

"Yes, the story for Ruth. She'll come by sometime today, asking about her darling son and to check on the plumbing problems." I thought about her "darling son" lying wounded and cuffed to the heavy radiator upstairs, and I thought about the blood on her carpet.

I slipped on my black Keds and followed Officer Milby outside to the cruiser. I looked around nervously, but there was no one and nothing suspicious outside. Even if there had been, I somehow knew I'd be safe from here on out with this man by my side.

Chapter Fifty-Four

It was nearly five in the morning when we climbed in the police cruiser. It felt strange sitting up front with him. I considered asking him if I could roll down the window and smoke, but that probably would have been inappropriate.

"Okay, first off...Ruth is going to ask you if her son came and fixed your toilet. This is what I want you to tell her—he did come by and he did the work, but you thought he looked either high or drunk. She'll believe you, considering his history. Also, this will lower her suspicions about why he'll be missing for a couple days," he instructed. I nodded, amazed by Officer Milby's ability to make up stories on the fly.

"That brings me to my next point. It's possible that one of your neighbors saw my car parked outside last night. If they did, they might be the kind of neighbors that rat you out to your landlord. Therefore, if or when Ruth asks you about it, stick with the story about the panic attack. Tell her you called 911 because you thought your heart was going to explode. Act embarrassed about it, and she'll stop asking questions."

He thought for a minute and added, "Let's just hope no one saw 'Albuquerque Police Department' written across the side of my cruiser. We'll park close to the side of the building at the motel, and pray no one tries to read where it's from. We can't hide the fact that I'm here for long."

"Okay," I said, taking in all of the details. "What else?" I asked, racking my brains for any other missed details.

"Well, then there's me. Ruth's going to find out there's a man staying at your house. Somebody will see me. So, let's just tell her I'm an old boyfriend from Albuquerque and I'm visiting for the week. If she asks what I do for a living, tell her the doctor story I told you earlier—only this time leave out the part about me ditching med school and joining the police force."

We pulled into the back parking lot of a dark, dingy motel called Maxine's Hideout. It had been here all my life, and I remembered driving past it a hundred times as a youth. "I'll be in and out," Officer Milby said, climbing out of the car. He locked the doors behind him.

I sat in the passenger seat, watching him disappear through the doors of the guest office. Despite all of tonight's excitement, I couldn't stifle a yawn. I was exhausted. I looked at the clock on the dash. It was 6:03 a.m. It suddenly dawned on me that I had to be at work in less than three hours.

I was going to have to call in today. I wondered if I was going to lose my new job over all of this…

Officer Milby jumped back in the car, holding a ragged key card for room sixteen. He grinned at me sheepishly. "I feel slimy just walking in that place," he admitted. I told him about my work schedule.

"You have to go to work, Wendi. I know you're tired, but you need to behave normally right now. We can't give anyone cause for concern," he explained.

"But I have to be there in less than three hours!" I protested.

"I'll watch over you while you nap, and then I'll wake you at 8:20," he said matter-of-factly. Not only did I have less than three hours to sleep, but since we had to leave the police cruiser parked at the motel, we still had a twenty-minute walk ahead of us.

We walked through the streets of Flocksdale silently. Despite all of the evening's drama, I was exhausted. I needed a nap, even if it was only for a brief period of time.

As we finally approached the house, I yawned again. "What are you going to do while I'm working?" I asked quizzically.

"Question our suspect. Duh," he said, winking at me.

Chapter Fifty-Five

With merely a half hour of rest, I stumbled into my morning shift at McDonald's. My face was puffy from lack of sleep, and there were bluish-black circles under both of my eyes. Andrea looked at me, raising her eyebrows questioningly. Officer Milby had warned me that we didn't want to raise suspicion, and the fact that I looked hung over this morning certainly didn't help my cause.

"I had a hard time sleeping," I told her honestly.

"Do you want to work in the back today? Wash dishes and do some prep work?" she asked, sounding concerned.

"Sounds fantastic," I said, trying my best to smile. If I'd been worried before about my new supervisor suspecting that I was using again, I was definitely concerned now. After this was all over with, I was going to have to get a new job.

I stood in front of the long, metallic sink, using a hose to spray food particles and condiment residue from the surfaces of the trays. One of them was covered in ketchup, and I watched the red, gelatinous substance flow down the sides of the tray and drip into the wide basin of the sink. It reminded me of Zach's blood.

My stomach was tied in knots all day. I wondered about Officer Milby and Zach. What was going on at that house? It was such a struggle, going about my day like it was any other day, all the while holding onto the knowledge that someone was being held captive at my house. I wanted to just say, 'Fuck it' and walk out of there, but I had to stay the full day. I needed the money and I needed to behave normally, according to Officer Milby.

Around noon, a short, freckle-faced teenager came to the back to get me. By then, I was chopping tomatoes and onions at the prep table that stood near the walk-in freezer. Every time someone opened the door, I was hit with a rush of cool, crisp air, and it felt like a relief on my nervous, sweaty skin.

"There's someone here to see you," my young coworker told me, a singsong quality to her voice. Who the hell had come to my work to see me?

I took off my apron and made my way to the front. I'm not sure why I was surprised to see Ruth, leaning against the rack of condiments. Officer Milby warned me she was going to come, but I guess I hadn't expected her to turn up at my place of employment, and certainly not so soon. I smiled at her cheerily—secretly sick inside—not wanting to see or speak to her at all. I considered running out the restaurant doors, catching the next bus out of

Flocksdale. If I ever managed to get back out of this town, I was never coming back.

Ruth was wearing a red and green flannel shirt that reminded me of a Christmas tree, her hair pulled up in a messy bun. Some women look spectacular with messy hairdos, but I have never been one of them. As much as I wanted to run, I remembered Officer Milby's instructions, and I walked up to Ruth with a pleasant expression plastered on my face.

"How's it going? Are you here to eat lunch?" I asked, trying to play it off coolly.

"Actually, I wanted to check in with you regarding the plumbing issue and ask you about my son," she said, a grave expression on her face.

"Let me see if I can take my lunch break," I told her, walking around to the back.

I asked my boss if I could go on break. It was almost rush hour, and we normally had to wait until before or after the busy hours to take our breaks, but she said okay, looking at me again with that pitiful expression of hers. I wondered if Andrea was starting to regret hiring me in the first place. I was certainly turning out to be a burden, if I did say so myself.

I grabbed a bottle of water and headed out to the lobby to talk to Ruth. She was already sitting at a small table near the back of the restaurant. I sat down across from her and took off my sweaty ball cap. But then I thought about my mother's recent visit to the restaurant, and quickly slipped it back on.

"Did my son show up to fix your toilet last

night?" she asked, getting straight to the point.

I nodded. "Yep, he did. He had to run a snake through it to unclog it and he replaced a part in the back, I think." Lies. They flowed off my tongue so easily, which was disconcerting. Sometimes I frightened myself.

"Is everything working fine now?" she asked.

"Yes. No more problems," I said.

"I told Zach to call me last night when he finished, bringing me up to date, but he never did. Then his boss from the plumbing company called me at home this morning, said he didn't show up at his first job site this morning with his usual crew. I went to Zach's house, but nobody was home," she explained, wringing her hands together worriedly.

I stared at her.

"I know you don't know my son, but did he mention anything to you about where he was going?" she asked hesitantly. *More lies coming...*

"Well, I didn't want to say anything, Ruth...but you know my past with my parents, and I thought I detected alcohol on his breath. His pupils were also dilated. I got the feeling he might have been drinking and possibly high on drugs," I stated matter-of-factly.

Ruth looked at me, her expression unchanging. "That's what I was worried about. I had a feeling something like this was going on...anytime he misses work, it's usually because he's getting high again." She tossed her hands up in exasperation.

"I'm sorry, Ruth. I know it wasn't my place to tell you..."

"No! Thank you for telling me, dear. I appreciate

your honesty and your friendship," she said, patting me on the hand. *If you only knew*, I thought miserably. I had no doubt that Ruth and I would never be friends, at least not in this lifetime.

"Well, I'll let you get back to work. Hopefully, I'll hear from Zach in a day or two after he's done with whatever type of binge he's on this time," she said, gathering her purse and standing up.

"Ruth...one more thing. There's this guy I used to date in Albuquerque. His name is Jonathan. He came to town to see my new place and pay me a visit. He's only staying a couple days, but I wanted to let you know."

Ruth still looked like she might cry about the news of her son. "Oh, that's fine, honey. I don't care about that. I'm glad you have someone to keep you company," she assured me. I watched her leave, feeling a sense of relief that I'd gotten that over with, but overcome with dread. Eventually, Ruth would find out the real truth, or she may even be involved in what happened to me, and I didn't want to be there when she did.

Chapter
Fifty-Six

When I walked inside my home, I heard the unmistakable sounds of metal clanging against stone. I stood still in the doorway, wondering if the house was still safe. Surely, Officer Milby didn't let our prisoner escape?

But then I heard the sounds of metal scraping again. They were coming from the cellar below. "Officer Milby?" I called out.

"I'm downstairs," he answered in a tired, gravelly voice.

I ventured down a few steps, my heart lurching with fear. Officer Milby was standing in a small clearing of dirt, maybe fifteen feet in diameter. He was digging up the basement floor! The area he was excavating was underneath the space where the washer and dryer had sat. He'd scooted the appliances out of his way.

He stopped digging and stood there, holding that shovel, looking at me tiredly. My eyes traveled around the room and I saw something that made my heart stop and my breath catch in my throat. Flashes of white and yellow objects, skinny yet long— bones.

"Is it her?" I asked, choking back the tears that were inevitably coming. I shook my head back and forth, not wanting to believe it could possibly be Claire down in that dirt.

"I found a bone that looks like a pelvis, and it has a distinct shape to indicate that it is most likely from a female…" But I was already racing back up the stairs, taking two at a time. I kept running, straight up to the second floor. Zach was still lying there on the floor, his hands and ankles shackled. There were food wrappers and empty bottles of water lying next to him.

"Are you kidding me? You were actually feeding this pig?" I screamed, and then I started hitting and punching at Zach again. "Who killed her? That plump, manly bitch! I know she did it! Who is she?" I bellowed, digging my nails into his fleshy cheeks.

Zach jerked back and forth, screaming, trying to escape my attack. I shouted wildly, a blood curdling, animal-like scream that frightened even me. I felt Officer Milby's thick arms grab me from behind. He wrapped them around me and lifted me off my feet, carrying me back down the stairs.

I tried to fight against him, kicking out my feet like an ill-tempered, unruly child, but then I finally went limp, accepting failure. When he let me go, I cried into his chest, beating my fists against him. He led me over to the couch, still holding me close.

I don't know why, but I felt like I was losing my best friend all over again. I didn't want to believe the harsh reality—that she'd been placed in the ground like a family pet...worse than a pet—like she was nothing, no one. The thought of her body being down there all this time, lying dead in that filthy dirt, was too much for me to bear. I pulled away from him, holding my head in my hands.

When I was calm, Officer Milby went back downstairs quietly. "I want to do this right. I'm collecting every bit of evidence I find, and digging up the entire floor to make sure I don't miss anything," he explained solemnly.

I should have helped him. It was the right thing to do. But I sat there on the couch, feeling dead inside, immobilized by my own devastation. I didn't turn on the TV or go upstairs to check on Zach. I just sat there, remembering that night in the house of horrors after Claire died, when I thought my body was going to grow as one with the couch beneath me. Maybe if I sat here long enough, it would finally happen this time.

Carissa Ann Lynch

Chapter
Fifty-Seven

After hours of staring at my dull living room, I got up to get something to drink. When I opened the refrigerator, I was surprised to find it filled with food. There was deli meat, Swiss cheese, ground beef, and fresh carrots with ranch dipping sauce. I opened the cabinets and stared at the shelves, which were filled with bread, chips, condiments, and canned soups.

I prepared sandwiches and placed a handful of carrots beside them on paper plates. I stood at the doorway to the basement, worried that if I entered, I'd lose my appetite completely.

"You want to come up and eat?" I called down, grimacing at the sounds of digging.

Seconds later, Officer Milby was standing upstairs, covered in grime and filth. His hands were covered in dirt and his face was smudged as well, like he'd been taking a nap in an old chimney chute. He scrubbed his hands in the sink with a small bottle of hand soap that I know I didn't put there. He saw me staring at it. "I got dish soap, shampoo, body soap, toilet paper, cleaning supplies, food…"

"Look, if you're trying to lecture me or make fun of me, just save it. I've been waiting to get my first check. I spent all the money I had moving into this place. And all the while, my dead friend was lying down there in the dirt…"

I turned away from him; I didn't want him to see my tears again. I took small bites of my sandwich, trying to focus on its taste instead of the pain that burned in my chest. Suddenly, he wrapped his arms around me from behind. My body tensed instantly.

Unlike earlier when he'd touched me, this felt more intimate and different somehow. Finally, I turned in his arms, facing him. A few years ago, I tried to kiss him, but he batted me away then. *This time he would have to kiss me himself*, I thought stubbornly. And that's when it happened. He leaned forward, pressing his lips to mine. For a moment we just stood there, enjoying our first real kiss.

It seemed so wrong, kissing him here with the prisoner upstairs and my dead friend below. Not to mention his dirty face and hands. *What a wonderful moment to have a sexy encounter*, I thought wearily. But he kissed me again and again, tender and sweet.

His lips were soft and sensitive, but needy and hungry all at once. I never wanted the kissing to stop. I didn't care about the bad timing or the grime on his skin. But he finally took a step back, his face reddening.

"I guess you can stop calling me Officer Milby," he said, rubbing the area around his mouth. His mouth was pink and splotchy from kissing. I wanted to kiss him again.

"Okay, *Jonathan*," I said, grinning up at him. But slowly my smile started to fade as I remembered the bones in the basement. "What did you find?" I asked, grimacing. "I'm ready to hear it." I motioned with my hands in a "give it to me" gesture.

"Two skull caps, the pelvic bone I told you about, and a bunch of random, small bones. It's not just Claire down there. There may be three or four bodies, maybe more…I can't be certain until I take it to a crime lab and have it all examined. The only good news is that we've finally found them. Their bodies can hopefully someday be returned to their families. The bad news is that the bodies are so badly decayed that I wonder if DNA testing is even possible."

"So, we may never even know who they are. And there's no evidence of who actually did this to prove my story," I answered gloomily.

"That's why we're going out tonight to get our own evidence," he replied firmly.

I raised my eyebrows skeptically, wondering what exactly he had in mind.

Chapter Fifty-Eight

Jonathan wanted to scour the neighborhood, and with my help, gather as much information about possible suspects and crime scenes in the neighborhood. That all sounded well and good, but what good did it do us when we didn't have a car? Jonathan's police cruiser was still parked in the lot of Maxine's Hideout. As though reading my thoughts, he said, "I have a rental car parked down the street. How do you think I got all the groceries and the shovel?" he asked, smiling at me goofily.

I stared at him, dumbfounded. "Okay, let's go," I said, grabbing my backpack. "First, let me check on our prisoner and take a five minute shower," he said, taking off upstairs. I didn't hear any talking going on, and he reappeared less than ten minutes later, his shirt still damp from his freshly washed hair. He smelled like fruity girl soap mixed with his own natural, manly scent. I took a deep whiff of him, fighting the urge to kiss him again.

"Zach still hasn't talked, by the way," he said, breaking my longing stare.

"Not even a word?" I asked, disbelievingly.

"Nope. Besides his initial accusation toward you, he's refusing to speak with me. I think he knows that I don't believe his bullshit and he's not too eager to incriminate himself at this point."

Jonathan slipped on a light jacket and we left the house, making our way toward an old Ford pickup down the street. It was parked underneath a hazy street lamp, and it certainly looked like it belonged there. I doubted that any of the neighbors were too worried about an old truck parked in the street.

The truck looked like it'd been through the ringer, with a row of dents down its side and a faded paint job. I started to make a joke, but then Jonathan warned, "Don't you say anything bad about my Ford. I begged for this at the rental place." He grinned at me cheerily and I made a zipping motion across my lips.

I climbed in the passenger seat beside him. The inside of the truck was just as worn out as the exterior, but somehow, it seemed to fit Jonathan perfectly. The first thing he did was open up the glove box to reveal a set of expensive looking binoculars and a pair of Maglites. He also had a couple boxes of ammunition and a handgun in there. I'm not normally a huge fan of guns, but I felt relieved seeing it there.

"Where to now?" I asked eagerly.

"I'm going to ride up and down each street. I want you to point out any houses you recognize, think you might know for certain, or any that cause you suspicion or general unease."

"Gladly," I said, pulling my seatbelt across my lap.

I immediately pointed out the spot on my own street where I'd gotten inside the limousine with the man named Jed. Moments later, I also pointed out the narrow dirt road where I'd been dropped off wearing the blindfold after being kidnapped.

That's when I remembered the ten minute time frame that I'd timed out in my head. "The house where I was held captive was exactly a ten minute drive from where they dropped me off, right here," I told him. Jonathan looked at me, confused.

I explained to him what I meant, and how I'd counted the seconds in my head. Just as I had earlier, he pointed out that it was possible the driver had driven in circles to confuse me and throw me off from the real location. "I know," I said, nodding. "I already thought of that."

"However, I don't think your captors were that smart."

"Why do you say that?" I asked, furrowing my brows at him.

"Because they let you go," he said softly. "They definitely underestimated your tenacity and resiliency." I smiled to myself, enjoying the flattery. "And I don't think they took the time to drive in circles to confuse you," he added.

Jonathan suddenly stopped the truck, pulling over to the side of the dirt road. "What speed do you reckon you were going?" he asked.

"Huh?"

"How fast was the car going that you were

traveling in?" he asked patiently.

"How should I know?" I asked, frustrated.

"Close your eyes and think about it," he pressed me. I did close them, thinking back to that hellish day. I was scared to death, only a child, and I didn't believe they were truly letting me go. I was certain they were taking me somewhere to kill me. It took forever for them to stop, and I remember that it felt like a slow, torturous drive...

"We were going really slow," I said finally.

"About this slow?" Jonathan asked, and I realized the truck was moving again. I kept my eyes closed.

"A little bit faster," I said. He picked up speed.

"Tell me when it feels right," he urged.

"Now," I said, moments later. I kept my eyes closed, riding in silence, trying to focus on the speed and vibrations of the vehicle.

Minutes later, Jonathan stopped the truck again. I opened my eyes. I didn't recognize the street we were on. "Where are we?" I asked, looking at him nervously. "If your driver came from this direction and stayed in this neighborhood for ten minutes approximately, then the house where you were held captive should be nearby, probably on this street."

Chapter
Fifty-Nine

"What's the name of this street?" I asked, my breath catching in my throat. It felt like something heavy and horrible was lying on my chest, making it impossible for me to breathe comfortably. "This is Clemmons Street, three streets over from where Zach supposedly lives on Weston," he stated.

It all made perfect sense. I thought about my phone conversation with Ruth, her telling me that her ex-husband, Hank, and stepdaughter, Jennifer, moved into a house in the same neighborhood as her and her boys: a street named Clemmons Street. I'd looked for it that day in the rain, but when I saw the tarp-covered limo on Weston Street, I'd run away as fast as I could.

Jed had taken us to Hank's mother's house initially, and that's where we gave Jennifer the drugs, but it made perfect sense that she and Hank—aka Garrett—would bring me to their own home. But someone had buried the bodies at the house Ruth lived in back then with her two sons…

I considered everything that I knew so far, and that's when I realized—James and Zach must have done the burying. They made the two young boys do all of the risky endeavors—luring in the girls and disposing of their bodies afterwards, all the while the adults got to have all the fun and make money off of me. I was overcome with feelings of disgust and hatred. Somewhere, deep down, I almost pitied the two boys. They were kids too, being taken advantage of and used by adults who they thought they could trust. Just like me and Claire.

I still wanted to kill Zach for what he did, even if it wasn't completely his fault. Nothing could bring my friend back, and someone had to pay for what was done to her.

Jennifer and Hank were making money from the men who abused me. How many other girls had they done this to over the years? I sunk down in the passenger's seat, wondering how responsible my silence truly was for their rapes. And some of their murders, I reminded myself, thinking about the bones in my basement.

"Wendi?" Jonathan was calling out my name, but I was staring straight ahead through the windshield, the road before me hazy and endless. "Get it together. I need you to focus," he said, reaching over to squeeze my shoulder lightly.

I took a breath. Willed my eyes to focus and my heart to stop pounding inside of my chest. I looked at several houses on each side of the street, studying their structure and the sense they gave me. A few of them were two-story dwellings, but none had boarded up windows, and they didn't look right to me.

"I don't think these are it," I said finally, hating to disappoint Jonathan and feeling disconcerted myself.

"Let's drive down a little farther. There are a few houses down at the end of this street. I think this is a dead end road," he murmured thoughtfully.

The truck lurched forward and I focused intensely on each house we passed. We were reaching the end of the street. The house at the very end was a rundown Victorian home. It was shrouded in darkness. I don't know why, but I felt drawn to it—in an inexplicable, creepy sort of way.

"I don't see any boarded up windows..." Jonathan said, cutting into my thoughts.

"Look! There's a flood wall behind it and a narrow alley between it and the back of the house!" I said, leaning forward in my seat.

"Does that mean something to you? A flood wall?" he asked excitedly. I shook my head.

"No, but it means we can go around somehow and look at the backside of the house. I can't be certain from here if this is the house, but another view might help. There has to be an alleyway, or something between it and the flood wall," I commented.

Jonathan backed up the truck, using an adjacent driveway to turn us around. I don't know why, but as we pulled away, I almost got the feeling that the windows of the house behind me were watching— like evil, menacing eyes—following my every movement.

Chapter Sixty

Jonathan placed a comforting hand on my knee as he pulled away from Clemmons Street and circled back around to the barely passable alleyway behind the dilapidated Victorian home. There was, in fact, an alleyway between the old house and the flood wall, and we rode down the alley slowly, approaching the backside of the structure. There was a tall flood wall to our right, and it was covered in illegible graffiti.

Jonathan stopped the truck directly behind it. So much for not looking suspicious, I thought, staring up at the big, ugly house. Sure enough, there was a boarded up window on one of the first floor rooms. My eyes drifted upward to the room directly above it. There were two, tiny, square windows, just like the ones I'd seen in the room on the second floor that was mine.

I stared at the windows, more certain than ever. "That's why there was never any light coming through…" I spoke aloud, but I was mainly talking to myself.

"Why?" Jonathan glanced my way. "Talk to me," he begged.

"Claire couldn't see anything through the boards that were covering her window and it was always dark on the other side of my window too. It always looked like nighttime outside from my point of view in the room. It makes sense now…the flood wall was blocking out the daylight."

"Are you sure this is it?" he asked quietly.

"Positive," I said, keeping my eyes locked on the house of horrors.

Despite its decrepit appearance, the house didn't seem to hold as much fear for me now as it had as a child. I knew the people inside it were evil and cruel, but they were also weak-minded and pathetic. Anyone who could hurt a child—or *children* I should say, because I wasn't the only one—was an absolute coward. "I'm not afraid of cowards," I said aloud, staring at the house intently.

Jonathan squeezed my hand. "I know you're not. You are very strong, Wendi," he said softly. I kept my eyes on the house, but I was grateful for his kind words. Hearing someone call me by my real name again was incredible. Jonathan opened his middle console and pulled out an official looking Polaroid camera. He snapped several photos from where he sat in the driver's seat.

"Can you arrest them yet?" I asked breathlessly.

"We still have work to do. Tomorrow night is Friday and I want to post up at the skating rink, see if we can gather any more information before we present the case to the local police. I also want to question Zach some more. Maybe now that I know where the house is, he'll cave and give me some more information."

"God, I hope so," I said. My entire body was trembling, but it wasn't from fear anymore. I was angry beyond belief. I couldn't wait to get these scumbags. Jonathan put the truck in reverse and backed down the alleyway slowly. Just as he was pulling out, I spotted two shiny headlights coming down Clemmons Street. We were headed in the other direction, but I kept my eyes fixated on the passenger's side mirror. I stared at the reflection, focusing on the beacons of light.

The headlights belonged to a mid-sized two-door vehicle, and it was pulling into the front driveway of the Victorian home. "It's them! Someone's pulling in! Turn around!" I shouted to Jonathan.

"Wendi, we can't just run up on the house and start making accusations…" But I didn't get to hear him finish, because I jumped out of the slow moving truck, and I took off on foot, running toward the house of horrors.

Chapter Sixty-One

I raced back up the alleyway, stopping abruptly at the back of the house. Where I stood now, I was only a few steps away from the room Claire died in. I wasn't ignorant enough to go inside the house, but I had to see who was getting out of that car. I had to see their faces. I needed to know who lived here, and see if I could match any faces to those I remembered.

I crept around the side of the house, edging up to the front corner, just as I heard the sound of two car doors opening and closing. Before I could even peek around the corner at their faces, I felt two big hands grabbing me from behind. I started to scream, but the sound was muffled by a hand placed over my mouth.

"It's me," Jonathan whispered in my ear. "Don't scream or they'll catch us."

I nodded, my heart racing so fast I thought it would burst through my chest. Together, we peered around the corner, just as three figures were heading through the front door. I saw their faces only briefly—a quick flash—and then they were gone.

"Let's go," Jonathan said, leading me by the elbow back down the alley to the truck. "We'll find out who lives there and get a search warrant. It was just too dark," Jonathan said, starting up the engine and looking at me sadly.

"It may have been dark, but I recognized all three of them," I said, my voice quivering.

He looked at me incredulously. "Who were they?" he asked, driving the truck away from Clemmons Street.

"Jennifer, the one who called herself Jeanna. Hank, the one she referred to as Garrett. And the other man, I don't know his name, but I knew his face."

Jonathan looked at me, waiting for me to explain more about the last man. "I saw a lot of men in that house. I don't know them by name, only the way they looked…and smelled," I finished, staring down at my sneakers. Without saying a word, he sped up angrily, barreling down the streets of Flocksdale, taking out his anger on the roads.

Despite Jonathan's anger, I couldn't help but smile. Even though it was terrifying seeing the house and my captors again, I felt a deep sense of self-satisfaction because now I knew where the monsters were. They'd been haunting my dreams for so long I was starting to wonder if they were real anymore…if they'd ever been real in the first place. Now I knew they were, and I knew just where to find them.

***

I was ready to go home after that, but Jonathan was revved up and ready to investigate. After leaving the house on Clemmons Street and throwing his little tantrum, Jonathan rode down to Weston Street. I pointed out the house with the covered limousine. "That must be where Jed lives," I told him.

"This is definitely not where our buddy Zach lives," Jonathan stated matter-of-factly.

"How do you know where Zach lives?" I asked.

"I looked at the identification in his wallet. Lucky for you, he doesn't appear to have a driver's license. If he had, he would have driven to your house the other night, and then you would have been stuck with his vehicle in your driveway. What would you have done if I hadn't shown up? Just admit that you need me..." he joked, giving me a smug sideways glance.

"Where does Zach live?" I asked, not in the mood for Jonathan's humor. He looked up and down the street.

"About five houses down from here," he said pointedly. "But what I'm concerned with now," he said, pointing straight ahead, "is figuring out if this is really where Jed lives."

I stared at the shabby clapboard house with the covered limo in the back. There was definitely someone home in there because it was lit up like Christmas morning. Suddenly, the front door to the house swung open right on cue, and a middle aged man with a beard came barreling through it unsteadily. At first I thought we'd been spotted, but then I saw his mouth moving, and I realized he was shouting back at someone inside. He said something else, and then stumbled over to a white sedan on the street in front of his house.

The man looked like he might be drunk. I figured he was going out for a drive, but then he simply reached inside the driver's side door and retrieved what appeared to be a pack of cigarettes. He pulled the plastic wrapper off the top and ripped off the cellophane, glancing around the neighborhood sketchily. I thought for sure he was going to spot us. For a moment, his head even turned in our direction and he appeared to be staring straight at us, but then his eyes shifted away, and he headed back toward the entrance of the house.

My heart was beating rapidly now. I knew who he was. At first I hadn't been certain, but then I'd seen his eyes clearly in the pale moonlight, and I'd known beyond a shadow of doubt. I knew those eyes well; I'd never forget them—staring back at me in the rearview mirror of the limo. I wasn't sure what his real name was, but in another life, he'd called himself Jed.

I was pretty sure that not only had Jed been the one who'd driven me to my first meeting with Jennifer, but that he'd also been the one who drove me to the spot where I'd been dumped afterward, blindfolded. Earlier, when my eyes were closed and I was imagining that ride in the backseat blindfolded, I'd remembered smelling something musty and dank in my seat. It was the same aroma that hit me when I'd climbed inside Jed's limo with

Claire and the two boys the first time.

I shivered, goose bumps popping out all over my arms and calves.

"He's talking to a woman in the doorway," Jonathan said, lifting the binoculars to his face.

"Let me see!" I demanded, yanking them out of his hand. "Sorry," I whispered, lifting the lenses over my eyes.

The woman standing next to Jed—if that was even his real name—was the short, plump woman I'd seen wrestling with Claire right before she was killed. She was also the one who'd drug Claire's lifeless body back in the room, so she quite possibly was the one who'd killed her. Honestly, it didn't matter who did what anymore. They were all guilty in my mind. Guilty as sin.

"Do you recognize either one of them?" Jonathan asked steadily.

"It's Jed, the limo driver. And the woman was there in the house too. I'm pretty sure she helped commit Claire's murder." He immediately lifted his cameras lens, zoomed in, and started snapping more photos.

***

On the drive back to the rental house, or "the burial site" as I'd come to think of it, he asked me more questions about the people I'd seen in the house. "I didn't see many of the faces of the men who came in the room, like I said. It was dark and I think I was unconscious or seriously doped up for most of it…"

243

The look he gave me made me cringe. "Please don't look at me like that. I don't want your pity," I told him firmly.

"I'm sorry this happened to you, Wendi," he said hesitantly.

I nodded, looking away out the passenger window. The houses became blurry as my eyes began filling with tears. I held them open wide, struggling to keep the tears from spilling over my eyelids. "I'm going to get them for you," he said, reaching out to take my hand. "I promise you I will. I couldn't protect you then, but I will now…"

I thought about the egg. Falling over the edge, making a successful landing to the ground.

"Thank you," I told him. "Thank you for everything you're doing to help me." I let the tears spill over, feeling a rush of relief. I thought about Jonathan's promise the whole ride home, and even though it was hard to believe, I wanted to trust in him. If anyone could rescue Wendi Wise and bring these monsters to justice, it was him.

Chapter Sixty-Two

"All I want to do is take a shower. Wash all the grime and filth away, everything that I've seen and had to think about tonight," I told Jonathan, plopping down on my living room couch.

"Go take a shower," he coaxed me, massaging my shoulders gently.

"I don't want to take a shower with him upstairs," I said, referring to our prisoner. "I don't want to be naked with him anywhere in the vicinity. I know that sounds stupid," I muttered.

"It doesn't sound stupid. I'll stand guard outside the door. I need to give him more food and water, anyway. Maybe put a towel under him because he's probably shit his pants by now," he said, wrinkling up his nose.

"I know you're the police. But we need to go to the local police with this. We can't hold him here forever. We know all the major players now, and we can give the police their addresses. We'll tell them my story. We have dead bodies in the basement. The longer we wait, the greater chance we take of losing evidence or being unable to obtain DNA. And I know it seems fishy—the fact that I'm renting the house where the bodies are buried—but I just started renting this place. No one in their right mind would believe those old skeletons were put there by someone who just moved in here. With search warrants, you guys will definitely find more evidence in their homes. Possibly find more bodies... Hell, Ruth might even be involved, as much as I don't want to believe that. I'm pretty sure her husband, Charlie, was one of those men who—" I couldn't finish the sentence. He squeezed my hand assuredly.

"I agree with you completely, and you're starting to sound like a cop yourself," he said, chuckling slightly.

"Promise you'll guard the door?" I asked, sounding and feeling smaller than I'd like.

"Yes. And as soon as you get out of the shower, we're going to drive down to the local police department and tell them everything," Jonathan said firmly.

"Really?" I asked, feeling a glimmer of hope from somewhere deep inside me.

"Really," he said, wrapping his arms around me. "Now go wash up. You're smelly." He winked at me flirtatiously.

Our prisoner was asleep and still firmly attached to the radiator. I headed into the bathroom, locking the door behind me. I double checked the lock three times. Jonathan took his post, leaning against the wall next to the doorway. I knew beyond a shadow of a doubt that he would keep me safe.

I turned the shower on and started stripping off my clothes. The water was hot, but I wasn't ready to get in yet. I stood in front of the full length mirror that was nailed to the back of the door, letting the room fill with steam. I stared at myself in the mirror until the glass turned foggy, making me disappear. "Have you seen this girl?" I whispered, staring at the blurry shape of my face in the mist.

I'd barely been intimate with a man since childhood, and I still felt uncomfortable looking at my own naked body. I wiped the condensation from the mirror and continued to stare at it, forcing myself to examine the contours of my body. For the first time in a long time, I felt genuine desire for a man. I wanted to lay naked with Jonathan and feel him touch me sweetly. I placed my hands on my breasts, imagining they were his hands. But then I imagined cruel, rough hands grasping me in the darkness, and I suddenly wasn't so sure.

I pressed my body against the door, knowing that Jonathan was right there waiting, only inches away from me on the other side. I wanted to kiss him and press my face into his chest again. I never wanted to feel unsafe again.

I stepped under the shower head, eager to wash the darkness away. The strawberry shampoo and body wash that Jonathan bought me were propped up on the soap tray. I squirted a dollop of shampoo on my palm and started scrubbing my hair thoroughly. My body felt heavy from lack of sleep and exhaustion from today's stressful excursion. I yearned to have a bath tub.

I know it sounds strange, but I plopped down on the floor of the shower, letting the water consume me. The water from the shower head formed its own little trickling dome of water around me. It felt like a protective shield. I closed my eyes, my thoughts drifting back to a memory of me in a bathtub at that Victorian home. I was slumped down in the sudsy water and Jeanna—Jennifer—was leaning over me, pouring warm water over my head. She'd been gentle as she bathed me. She'd talk or hum while she did it, feigning motherliness.

It made me sick to think of it. I opened my eyes, thinking about something she'd said: "I'm sorry, darling. It's almost over. If it was up to me, you wouldn't be here. We just do what we're told…" By 'we' had she meant her and Hank? If she wasn't making the calls, then who was? Was there something even bigger going on here? Was there some sort of kingpin pulling the strings?

I jumped out of the shower, drying off with one of Ruth's holey towels she'd left behind. I needed to stop Jonathan from contacting the police just yet. If we turned them all in now, we might never know the whole, complete truth behind it all. We needed to go to the skating rink and the plaza. I had no clothes to put on besides the dirty, crumpled clothes on the wet floor, the ones I'd worn previously.

"Screw it," I said, wrapping my towel around me tightly.

I opened up the bathroom door, letting the steam roll out. Jonathan wasn't guarding the door as promised. I stood there, temporarily dumbfounded by his absence. I stared straight ahead at the radiator. Jonathan wasn't the only one missing. Zach was no longer cuffed to the radiator.

Chapter Sixty-Three

Our prisoner was gone, his shackles lying limply on the floor next to the massive blood stain beneath where he'd been lying when I stabbed him. I stood there, frozen, unsure of what to do. How did he get away? And where the hell was Jonathan?

It suddenly occurred to me that I was in serious danger. I didn't know how or what exactly was going on, but I knew it was something bad. Since there was no way I was walking downstairs into the darkness below, I ran back in the bathroom and slammed the door shut behind me. I locked it securely, backing up from the door.

I held my breath, listening for sounds downstairs or any sort of clue as to where Jonathan and Zach had gone. I didn't hear any sounds of struggle. I crept forward and pressed my ear to the door; I closed my eyes, trying to hear something, anything…

Fear began to overtake my body, and I felt short

of breath. The next thing I knew I was panting, and the sound of my own heartbeat pounded in my ears, making me want to scream. Only a few minutes ago, I'd felt completely safe, knowing that Zach was securely fastened to the radiator, and Jonathan was waiting at the door.

I pressed my ear to the door again, listening to the silence.

"I hear you breathing," said a voice on the other side of the door. I jumped back, struggling to suck in breaths, but I couldn't get my lungs to fill. That voice...

The voice did not belong to Jonathan or Zach. It didn't even belong to a man. The voice on the other side of the door belonged to someone I knew very well. A voice long gone, but never forgotten. It was Claire.

Chapter Sixty-Four

"You didn't really think I was dead, did ya?" said the voice, letting out a low, gurgled chuckle. The tone of the voice sounded deeper and different, but I still knew it was Claire. What in God's name was going on? Was I truly losing my mind?

For a moment, I wondered if I was still in that apartment in Albuquerque, hiding in that closet, tweaked out on meth. Maybe everything else had just been some long, drawn out trip…maybe I was completely insane and always had been.

Shut up! screamed a voice from inside me. *You aren't crazy and you aren't high this time.* "What's going on, Claire? I don't understand," I said, still standing back from the door. My hands were shaking uncontrollably, and I dropped my towel to the ground.

"Open the door and I'll tell you everything," Claire said, a sickening sweetness to her tone. I instantly knew she was lying. I knew that something evil was going on here.

I briefly considered that maybe she was a ghost, back from the grave to haunt me. After all, she was supposedly buried in the floor of the basement…but I knew that wasn't the case. I didn't believe in ghosts or monsters. There were too many real monsters in this world to waste time worrying about supernatural ones.

This voice on the other side of the door was an older version of Claire, and it sounded less sincere. The realization that Claire was alive, standing on the other side of this door, was finally sinking into my psyche.

"Open the door or we're going to break it down, Wendi," came another voice from the other side. It was another female. I already knew who it was: Jennifer.

"Well, you're just going to have to break it down then," I said, stepping back and bracing for the attack.

But there was no response. I stood there, waiting for something to happen, but all I could hear was silence. I looked around the bathroom, trying to find something I could use as a weapon. The towel bar was already broken from my skirmish with Zach the other day. The only thing I could think to grab was a rubber plunger I'd seen sitting next to the toilet. I grabbed the plunger, clutching its useless handle. I held it out in front of me, waiting for them to break down the door. But nothing happened.

I backed up farther and farther from the door, waiting for the bathroom door to burst open. But suddenly, the linen closet behind me swung open, and someone yanked me inside of it.

Chapter Sixty-Five

Everything happened so quickly that I couldn't make sense of it all. Someone yanked me inside the linen closet from behind, and now I was being pulled down through a hole. I tried to grab onto something, but I was falling fast and hard, and nothing could slow me down.

I hit a rock hard surface, my body banging roughly against it as I let out a loud *oomph* sound. My head was spinning, but I looked around, realizing I was in the cellar of my rental house. *How in the hell did I get down here?* I wondered, struggling to stand up. I felt dizzy and confused.

Someone kicked me square in the chest, knocking me back to the floor. Zach's face loomed over me, twisted with hatred and anger. I was still naked from taking a shower, and he stared down at my nude body with a look of pure disgust. Despite the pain from his kick, I attempted to cover my breasts and private area.

"We grew up in this house, remember? We know all sorts of things you don't know about it," he declared, cackling maniacally.

"Yeah, like how our brother built a trap door in the basement that led up to the linen closet," Jennifer said smugly from behind him. I looked around for Claire but I didn't see her. Had I imagined her voice at the door?

It was the first time I'd seen Jennifer—aka Jeanna—since she'd let me go so long ago. She looked older now, with wrinkles forming at the corners of her mouth and eyes. But those evil eyes…there was no mistaking it, it was her—that evil bitch I'd never forget…

"Do you know why James built that trap door to the bathroom?" Jennifer asked, smiling down at me smugly. *This bitch was crazy. But I already knew that, didn't I?*

I shook my head no, my teeth chattering from the cold and sheer terror. "Because he wanted to find a way to sneak in there with me because we were in love," she boasted, staring down at me evilly.

"You were in love with your own brother?" I asked, choking out the words. Now it was her turn to kick me.

Her foot connected with my ribs, and I rolled onto my opposite side, howling in pain. I was certain that several of my ribs were broken. "James and I weren't brother and sister. My father had me before he ever met Ruth, and James had already been born, you stupid bitch!" she screamed defensively. The calm demeanor I remembered was gone.

I wanted to retort with a nasty remark, but I didn't want her to kick me again. My sides exploded with pain. Yes, something was definitely broken.

"Did you really think James cared about you? He didn't even tell you his real name! What did he tell you his name was, bitch?" When I didn't respond, she nailed me in the ribs with her foot again.

"Joey. He said his name was Joey," I choked, gasping for breath and clutching my bare side. "You were just a mark, a sucker...I let you live because he asked me to and because I thought you were just like the rest, but then he..." She looked away, her face contorting with angst. It was the most emotion I'd ever seen her display.

"When he jumped off the roof, he was holding that stupid necklace he'd given you in his hand. You're the reason he jumped, you stupid cunt! He was supposed to love me, not you!" she screamed. Suddenly, she was on top of me, punching me in the face over and over again. I put my hands up defensively, trying to fend her off, and I struggled to push up with my feet, lifting her weight off me.

But it was no use. She was much bigger and stronger, and my ribs ached painfully. "And after I let you go, you still had the nerve to show back up here. Did you think we wouldn't recognize you? How stupid can you be?" When I didn't answer she went on with her questions. "Were you coming back for him? Well, were you?" she screamed, bending down to grab a fistful of my hair. She pulled on it so hard that my vision went white and I screamed in agony.

"Get off of her. You look like a fool," said a female voice from across the room. One of my eyes was swelling shut, but with the good one I could see the image of my former best friend perfectly. Claire was standing across the room, near one of the spots where Jonathan had been digging. "I'm glad that's not me," she said, looking down at the hole where the bones were dug up. She kicked at the dirt and bones, smiling strangely.

Zach pulled Jennifer off of me, and I laid there on my back, staring at my old best friend. "How, Claire? Why? I don't understand—"

"You never understood anything about me, Wendi. I used to really like you, I really did. But blood is thicker than water, and I can't turn my back on family," she said with a careless shrug.

"What family?" I asked, tears rolling down my cheeks. The tears burned the skin on my cut, swollen face. Claire let out a cute, dainty laugh. It sounded just like the same laugh that echoed through the hallways of my house when she came over for sleepovers.

"You were my friend, Claire…"

"But they are my family," Claire said, pointing at Zach and Jennifer. "Didn't you ever wonder why I always wanted to stay at your house? Why I never invited you over? Jennifer is my cousin. Hank is my mother's brother. This has always been a family-run business, for generations! I was born into this, baby…"

"But you don't have to stay a part of it, Claire! You aren't like these people!" I yelled, holding my hand out pitifully toward my friend. I reached for her, my old best friend, the one I'd loved so much...but she looked at me with disgust and it reminded me of that other side of her, the one I'd only seen a few times.

"I still don't understand. We met Zach and James at the mall. They introduced themselves as Zeke and Joey, remember? I still don't believe any of this..." I moaned, rolling back over onto my side. I couldn't look at her anymore. "I watched you die, Claire..." I said, choking on my own sobs.

"You saw what you wanted, Wendi. It was all for show. My Aunt Betsy, the woman you saw dragging me across the room—we had it all planned out. If you thought I was dead, we knew you would be too scared to tell because you didn't want to get killed yourself or get your parents killed. We needed you to take us seriously, and keep your damn mouth shut. Plus, you never would have left that place if you knew I was still there. After you saw me downstairs through the vent, I had to play it off like I was a prisoner too."

Her words were like daggers, stabbing over and over again, piercing straight through the heart of me. I suddenly had a flash of memory—of Claire and her sister, Samantha, putting on Halloween makeup. They always wanted to dress up as something scary, and they both had a knack for making their faces look gory and realistically terrifying. You see what you want to see...I thought about her lying there, those lifeless eyes looking up through the grate, smears of blood and smudges of purple bruising on her face. Her face was destroyed. Bright red blood, like the color of paint. It was all fake…a big show, and I was the spectator. And Claire was enjoying every moment of it, then at the house, and here right now, I realized. As I looked at her standing over me, I realized she was still smiling. She enjoyed watching me suffer.

I thought about Zach, tied to the radiator that first night, saying, "You don't even know, do you?" as I begged him to tell me who killed my friend. He'd known all along that my friend was alive. What a sick, twisted trick. *And the joke was on me*, I realized, traumatized by this revelation.

I thought about the "Have You Seen This Girl?" flier, and all those online articles. Claire's name was mentioned in none of them. Not only was she alive all this time, but she never went missing in the first place. She probably confirmed the police reports that I'd run away. I imagined her standing next to my family, pleading for me to come home and giving them her condolences. I imagined her walking the halls at school, sulking because she lost her best friend and eating up the attention she received from it. I hated her more than I hated Jennifer, or any of the men that raped me. Unlike them, she was supposed to love me. She was my best friend.

Claire went on, "Just like my cousins, I helped recruit the girls. I never thought you would end up being one of our marks, but I didn't have a choice. None of us did. Maybe somewhere, way down deep, I felt a little regret, but I'm over that now. You weren't supposed to live, but Jennifer listened to James and she let you go, and we all almost went to prison because of it. You never should have come back to Flocksdale, Wendi…"

"Come on, guys! We need to get this over with!" shouted a voice from up above. Claire's sister, Samantha, came padding down the basement steps, peering at us mid-step.

"Now we really do have to put an end to this. This is the end, Wendi. You and your little cop boyfriend, we're going to put you in these holes and cover you up like all of the rest, and no one will ever find you," Claire said, clapping her hands together with glee. As her palms smacked together, I stared at her arms, still covered in those macramé bracelets. All this time, I had wondered what those letters spelled, and now I had a chance to find out. I squinted at the tiny beads with my one good eye. Seven letters. G-A-R-R-E-T-T. Garrett, a family name. The family from hell, I realized angrily.

"You should've just stayed gone, you silly bitch," Jennifer said, walking toward me slowly. She had a shovel in her hands.

"Wait! Where's Jonathan?" I screamed, suddenly fearing for his safety.

"I knocked him out with his own shovel. He didn't even see it coming. He was so focused on guarding you and keeping an eye on Zach that he never expected me to come charging up those steps," Claire said, smiling creepily.

I started to ask how they got inside the house, but then I realized that was a stupid question. They got the key from my landlord, Ruth. All this time, I thought I could lock up the doors and keep the monsters out. But they had a way in all along…my landlord, Ruth…another member of this horrible, macabre family.

"Don't worry, sweetheart. We'll put Jonathan in the hole on top of you after we've killed you both. You'll be together forever," Claire said, moving toward where I was lying on the floor.

Jennifer still stood over me, gripping the shovel tightly in her hands. She swung it back, preparing to bring it down on my head.

Chapter Sixty-Six

"Wait!" I screamed, holding my hands up over my head helplessly. "He didn't jump, Jennifer! That was all a lie!" I shouted desperately. I don't know where that came from; maybe I'd gotten so used to being a liar all of my life, that lies just flowed out of me naturally. Jennifer lowered the shovel a few inches, scrunching up her face thoughtfully.

"What are you talking about now, you stupid idiot?" she shouted, the shovel still gripped in her hands.

"I've been holding Zach prisoner here for days. He's been ratting out all of you to Officer Milby. He told us that he pushed James off the roof, and he planted the necklace to make everybody think it was a suicide! James never would have jumped, Jennifer. He didn't love me. He told me that he didn't love me. He said he was in love with someone else. He must have been talking about you!"

Everything was quiet for several seconds. I was grasping at straws here, and I knew it. Jennifer looked at me like I was crazy, but then she hesitated, her face contorting as her emotions changed. I could tell she was considering the validity of my claims. I honestly had no idea what happened to James that day. He could have been high and fallen, just like his mother claimed. But since he'd really been holding that necklace, then it probably was suicide over his guilt...but none of that mattered now because I had a story to sell. Even if it sounded unlikely, I knew she wanted to believe it. She wanted to believe that she was the one he loved, not me.

I decided my best bet was to just keep talking. "Zach was going to roll over on you and everybody. He was working with Officer Milby, helping him build a case against you guys and the rest of the family! Why do you think the local police haven't arrested him yet? Because he's their source of information! He's the one you should be after, not me!" I shouted.

I glanced nervously over to where Zach was standing. He was staring at me with a frightening snarl on his face as he took in my words. Suddenly, he came charging right toward me, and I knew he was going to kill me this time.

Chapter Sixty-Seven

I squeezed my eyes shut tightly, waiting for him to strangle me. This was it. They were finally going to put an end to my miserable, angst-ridden life.

But then I heard a loud clunk, and my eyes fluttered open confusedly. I saw Zach hit the floor with a thud. Jennifer had hit him over the head with the shovel. Zach groaned, pushing up to his knees groggily, but then she hit him again and again and again. Blood spurted from his mouth and nose, and then I heard the loud crack of his skull breaking.

Despite the pain, I managed to pull myself up to my feet. Even though I had temporarily distracted Jennifer, I knew they were still going to kill me. But getting rid of Zach gave me a better chance of surviving, because after all, three were easier to fight off than four. Adrenaline was racing through my body. I wasn't sure who I should go for first, but since Claire didn't have a weapon in her hand, I charged toward Jennifer first.

She was still hovering over Zach's body when I slammed into her, and she didn't even see it coming. I knocked her to the ground then went racing for the basement steps. Claire wasn't injured and she was much faster than me. I heard her screaming obscenities behind me. I was at the top of the stairs when Samantha appeared. She shoved me backwards, and then Claire reached for me from behind. The force of the shove caused my weight to slam into Claire, and we both went tumbling down the stairs, banging our bodies against the hard wooden steps. I was lucky enough to land on top.

I grabbed Claire by the hair and started slamming her head against the hard, stony surface of the floor. This time, she was going to get her head smashed in for real, courtesy of me. After everything she'd done, I hated her more than I'd ever hated Jennifer, or any of the men in the house of horrors.

But then I heard someone else behind me: either Jennifer had gotten up or Samantha was coming down the stairs. I looked up just in time to see metal smashing into my own face.

Chapter
Sixty-Eight

You know how those crazy cartoon characters always have floating stars around their heads on television? Well, I found out the hard way that "seeing stars" is not just a silly expression. Flashing specks darted across my field of vision and the room started to shrink, drifting farther and farther away.

"I should have killed you the first time, bitch," I heard Jennifer say, but her words sounded strange and distorted, like I was hearing them from the opposite end of a long tunnel, or from the bottom of a deep well. She was standing over me, preparing to hit me again with the shovel.

I wish Jonathan hadn't bought that shovel, I thought groggily, my mind not comprehending the gravity of this situation. Everything around me was spinning, like I was on a tilt-a-whirl. One time, Claire and I rode the tilt-a-whirl at Flocksdale's County Fair; we went around and around so many

267

times that she barfed on my new white shorts…my best friend was alive…my best friend was a stupid, lying, evil bitch and her family was going to kill me…

I waited for more metal to smash into my face, blood from my current head wound blurring my one good eye…*I was going to die*. After all this time, they were finally going to end this for good. The shovel came pummeling toward me again, and this time it hit me directly in the face. I felt my backside hit the cold, hard floor.

The ceiling above me swirled and swayed, and I struggled to retain consciousness.

I wasn't dead yet, but I would be soon if I didn't move. I tried to get up, but I saw her coming for me again. This was it. One more hit and she'd kill me for sure…but then suddenly, a loud bang rang out, reverberating in my ear.

"Flash bang! Game over…" I muttered, remembering a video game I used to play, my head spinning and spinning, the room getting smaller and smaller…then I was out, fading away completely. Everything went black.

Chapter Sixty-Nine

When I opened my eyes, I was lying on my back in a clean white room. *Is this Heaven?* I wondered curiously. But then I forced my eyes to focus, and I moved them back and forth, realizing I was in some sort of hospital room. There was a doctor standing at the end of the bed, looking at me warily.

"She's awake," he said with a thick foreign accent.

"Wendi! Honey!" a woman shouted, and I saw my mother's face. Was this really happening?

"You've been in a coma for several days, sweetie! But everything's going to be okay now. I have you back. And I'm never going to let you go," my mother gushed, tears flowing down her cheeks.

Lying on the bed beside me, she gripped me in her arms, soaking my own cheeks with her tears. The entirety of the room was coming into focus, and I could see two men standing on the other side of the bed, a few feet from where the doctor stood.

One of them was my father and the other one was Jonathan. They rushed over to each of my sides, reaching out for me. I had everyone I loved in one room. Suddenly, all of the darkness and emptiness I'd been feeling for years faded away, and I felt whole for the first time in my life. Landing: successful.

"It's over," I said. "It's really, truly over. This is the end…"

Epilogue

I wish I could tell you that my life went on to be perfect. That I went to college, got a fancy job, had a perfect marriage, and never used drugs again. But I am no longer a liar. My name is Wendi Wise, and I will never, ever be perfect. That is the truest statement I have ever made…I've been through some shit, and some of it I will never, ever be able to let go of. But I'm stronger because of all of it, and it has allowed me to tell my story.

In the end, Jennifer—aka Jeanna—was the one who got a smashed-in face. Jonathan woke up and blasted her right between the eyes with his .45, just in the nick of time. When he finished with her, he turned the gun on Samantha. She ran straight for him, wrestling for the gun like an idiot. He shot her in the leg, crippling her for life, but still letting her live. Zach died on that cold, cement floor of the cellar, a severe head injury inflicted by Jennifer's shovel. Ruth went from having one living son left to zero.

Claire survived as well. As it turns out, she was

the rat in the family, because in exchange for a reduced sentence, she rolled over on the whole Garrett clan, even her own parents and sister. Apparently, her family had ties with the mob. Her Uncle Hank—aka Garrett—owned the skating rink, plaza, and several other local establishments that were used as a front to kidnap and traffic children, sell drugs, and do God knows what else. Jed—his real name by the way—and his wife, Betsy—the one who "killed" Claire—also went to prison for life. Sometimes I wonder what happened to that old, creepy limo. Hopefully, it was compressed into a tiny cube and destroyed.

Jonathan saw the entire case through, and by the time it was all said and done, he'd discovered associations with the Garrett family that went all the way up to top government officials. Apparently, depravity exists in every neighborhood and across all socioeconomic lines.

Nearly thirty-six members of the Garrett family and its related partners were arrested, courtesy of my darling husband—Jonathan Milby. I can honestly say that I live with my very own version of a super hero—my husband. It's a wonderful feeling.

Thirty-six arrests is a great number. The number I don't like to think about are the dozens of bodies that were unearthed from the yards and basements of the Garrett family members. Bodies were in the basement at Ruth's rental house, as well as Jed and Zach's backyards. The majority of the bodies were found in a tight crawlspace that lay beneath the house of horrors. A black hole, filled with a sea of twisted limbs and battered skulls. Some of the remains were identified as local children. Some are still unknown.

I often lie awake at night, wondering why I'm not one of those bodies. I also wonder how many more girls died and were never found, their corpses thrown in the river behind the house of horrors. God only knows how many victims were really out there.

I also lie awake at night wondering how many of those deaths I could have stopped or prevented if I'd come forward sooner. But you know what they say about looking back…that you shouldn't unless you plan on going that way.

I never want to go back to being Elsie, the girl who hated herself and lived in her own prison. So now I simply take one day at a time, and I'm trying to forgive myself. I wasn't the one who killed them, and at the very least, I played a crucial role in bringing those killers to justice.

Speaking of bringing people to justice, Ruth and Charlie were also arrested, as well as Hank's elderly mother, Margie. Their exact roles in all this are unclear, but as it turns out, they knew enough about what was going on to make them all guilty as sin. Sometimes knowing something and doing nothing about it is just as bad as doing it yourself. I tried to feel sorry for them, but I simply couldn't anymore. I felt sorry for the innocent children and families they destroyed so long ago. They almost destroyed me and mine.

Several years ago, I wrote Claire a letter and sent it to the prison in Mooresville, which is where she spends her days now. In it, I told her that I'd forgiven her. She was a child that grew up amongst monsters, and inevitably, became one herself. I, of all people, understand what it's like to go through something terrible and then become a fuck-up because of it. For many years, I let the trauma of what happened in the house of horrors consume me, and it almost ate me whole.

I became a manager at McDonald's and Jonathan became a sergeant. We bought a house in Flocksdale. I never thought I'd want to live here again, but as it turns out, I love our little bungalow that sits on its own patch of grass. The skating rink was torn down, as well as most of the houses surrounding it. I can't say I minded that one bit. Jonathan asked me if I wanted to be there when that evil house on Clemmons Street was torn to the ground. My answer to that was a firm no. I know it's hard for him to understand, but I didn't want to be there; I didn't want to feel the presence of all those lost souls drifting away around me. I was at peace, and in my mind, that house and the evil inside of it died years ago when he rescued me from that hellish cellar.

My marriage to Jonathan has not always been easy, and I have relapsed a handful of times. But he and my family have stood by my side through all of the ups and downs, and I can honestly say that I finally know the meaning of true love. I no longer flinch when I feel the touch of his hands, and he was patient with me, giving me time to adjust to real intimacy.

My parents are old and graying now, and I love them more than I ever did before. I try to imagine what it must have been like for them, losing their only daughter for all those years. I know they feel a great deal of guilt over what happened to me, as though they could have prevented it. Like Jonathan, it's hard for them to completely understand that if it wasn't for them, I never would have made it. They taught me to be good, but strong, and the remembrances of them are what got me through those awful days in that house. They were amazing parents and still are; I don't know how they made parenting always seem so easy, but they did.

My dad is pushing seventy now, and was recently diagnosed with Parkinson's disease. His hands are too shaky to play the guitar anymore, but I've recently taken up lessons. I figure I could practice in front of him, maybe play him an old familiar Tom Petty song…

The year after Jonathan and I were married, we took a short trip to Albuquerque to visit an old friend. When I walked into Saint Mary's Home for Children, Miss Ally was bent over with her back toward me, tying a young girl's shoes. When she turned around and saw me standing next to Jonathan, her facial expression went from confused to worried, and then to excited to see me.

"Come here!" she squealed, clutching me in her aging, bony arms. I hadn't planned on crying, but I bawled into her chest. I told her everything and made amends.

I also made my amends to Remy. I sat at the base of her tombstone. Instead of flowers, I stuck one of our old Mad Lib books in the dirt beside her stone. If it wasn't for Remy, Jonathan never would have known the truth about what happened to me and who I really was. He never would have showed up that night in Flocksdale, and I surely would have died in that dirty, old cellar right next to Zach. Unlike Ruth, who knew what was going on with the Garrett family and did nothing about it, Remy took it upon herself to reach out and get the help I needed, but was too scared to get on my own. I will always be grateful for the actions she took that day.

My last amends were to Chuck and Baylor. Baby Claire was no longer a baby. Instead, she was a beautiful, smiling teenager. She seemed shy, but happy, and I was glad that I got to see that smile after all. Telling the Raffertons the truth was surprisingly hard, but I did it anyway. I apologized for disappointing them. They, in turn, apologized for disappointing me.

Even though I live far away in Flocksdale, I still talk to Baylor and Miss Ally nearly once a day. I need their advice often. Jonathan and I have a daughter of our own now, named Shelby. She's almost twelve. Being a good mother to her has proven to be the hardest job of my life, but I've loved every minute of raising her. Someday soon, when she's old enough, I'm going to tell her my story. But for now, I just let her be a silly, careless, teenage girl just like I once was. Maybe I'll never tell her. I don't want my darkness to seep through and saturate her life.

Just last week, Shelby went to the mall alone with friends. I didn't want to let her go, but at the same time, I know I can't lock her inside the house and make her my prisoner just because I want to protect her. There are all types of prisons in life, and I don't want my overly paranoid, protectiveness to be hers.

I said that I don't lie anymore—so now I'll tell the truth. I let her go to the mall, but she didn't go alone. I crept through the corridors of that old familiar plaza, watching her every move as she talked to boys and shopped for clothes. I had to be certain she was all right—I simply couldn't help myself.

Some nights, when I'm all alone, I pull out a copy of one of those old "Have You Seen This Girl?" fliers, the ones I keep hidden away in my drawer. I stare at the face of that little girl who had to endure so much. She was brave and strong. She didn't know it then, but she does now. The answer is: yes, I've seen her. I know her and I know her pain. But I also know her triumph and recovery. She is no longer lost. She has found her own little safe corner of the world, and she's sticking around this time.

The End

Acknowledgements

Thank you...

To my husband—You are my hero, my best friend, my confidant, my partner in crime.

To my children—Tristian, Dexter, and Violet—I love each and every one of you more than words could ever express. You are, by far, my greatest accomplishment. I'll be the first to admit that when it comes to being a mother, I'm still a work-in-progress. I hope to make you proud.

To Limitless Publishing—for taking a chance on me, for believing in Wendi's story, and for "getting" me as an author. Go Team Limitless!

To Ashley Byland at Redbird Designs and Jennifer O'Neill—for doing a fabulous job on the concept and cover art for this book. I fell in love with it instantly.

To the managing editor, Lori Whitwam—for breaking my heart gently when you told me I had to remove the Jim Morrison lyrics from this book, and for helping me so much during the pre-editing phase.

And a special thank you to my amazing editor, Toni Rakestraw—for fixing my mistakes and finding holes in the story I couldn't see, and for teaching me so much within a short amount of time.

To all of my family and friends—for supporting my dream and believing in me.

And thank you thank you thank you to all of my readers—you guys make all those sleepless nights and difficult editing rounds worth it.

About the Author

Besides my family, my greatest love in life is books. Reading them, writing them, holding them, smelling them…well, you get the idea. I've always loved to read, and some of my earliest childhood memories are me, tucked away in my room, lost in a good book. I received a five dollar allowance each week, and I always—always—spent it on books. My love affair with writing started early, but it mostly involved journaling and writing silly poems. Several years ago, I didn't have a book to read so I decided on a whim to write my own story, something I'd like to read. It turned out to be harder than I thought, but from that point on I was hooked. My first and second books were released by Sarah Book Publishing: This Is Not About Love and Grayson's Ridge. I'm a total genre-hopper. Basically, I like to write what I like to read: a little bit of everything! I reside in Floyds Knobs, Indiana with my husband, three children, and massive collection of books. I have a degree in psychology and worked as a counselor.

Facebook:
https://www.facebook.com/CarissaAnnLynchauthor

Twitter:
https://twitter.com/carissaannlynch

Goodreads:
https://www.goodreads.com/author/show/11204582
.Carissa_Lynch